THE BLUFF

K.D.J. WILLHOIT

— LUTIE HOLLOW —

THE BLUFF

Copyright © 2019 K.D.J. Willhoit

ISBN: 978-0-578-45523-5

All characters in this story are entirely fictional. Although locales, agencies and institutions may be factual, they are used in a fictitious manner without intent to describe their actual conduct or personnel.

Gratitude to Becky for proofreading and to Kathy, Hannah and Betty for their input and encouragement.

https://www.facebook.com/KDJWillhoit/

"It is never too late to be who you might have been."

- George Eliot

For Monica

❧ Prologue: Summer 1999 ❧

The Ferris wheel scared her more than any other ride. Though it didn't turn her upside down or fling her around like the Spider, the mere height was unnerving, particularly as it crested the top and started its descent. Her mind couldn't help but imagine a bolt breaking at the center of the spoke, sending her and her buddies rolling toward the ocean until the big wheel lost momentum and fell on its side. Nevertheless, every year someone always talked her into going up with them. Being afraid of the Ferris wheel was definitely grounds for being called a sissy. Mark was waiting at the bottom when she and Sarah disembarked. He had a fresh henna tattoo of a six-headed Mermaid on his bicep. He pointed to it, "Ricki, you wanna get one of these?" Ricki's stomach was still in her throat from the ride.

"Nah, I'll pass, unless they have Mermans?"

Mark looked perplexed. Her witty humor soared right over his head of black hair. They walked toward the livestock arena. The Lane County Fair was one of the largest in Central Oregon. The rodeo was a big attraction and people from as far away as Portland and Klamath Falls came to watch rider and bull get shaken down.

As the three teens approached the stands, Sarah noticed a cowboy sitting on top of a bull, poised for the eight-second ride. The bull seemed almost docile standing still in the pen, ears twitching futilely at flies. His large brown eyes stared at Sarah and she felt pity for him. She told him in her mind, "It'll be over soon and then you can go back to your stubble." On the rider's nod, the gate swung open and a half-ton of bucking fury exploded out the chute. Sarah had always wondered if these bulls truly objected to being ridden or were they trained to throw the rider for treats. She had heard that in Pro Bull Riding, bulls can win a place in a Hall of Fame and enjoy a wonderful retirement, siring hundreds of wannabe athletes. Mark cheered as the rider pulled himself up off the loose dirt, brushed himself off, turned to the crowd, put his hat on his head and his hand over his heart. The fans cheered, most of them already three beers down. Mark turned to talk to Sarah, but she was gone. Sarah had made her way over to the outgate where the gateman herded the spent bulls back into captivity. The bull she had pitied earlier came rushing into the gate, nostrils flaring. When adjacent to her, he came to an abrupt stop and nudged his nose between the horizontal bars that protected spectators from the stock. Instinctively, she stroked the smooth skin between his nostrils. The bull, amid all the commotion, seemed to be momentarily suspended. She smiled and said softly, "See, that wasn't so bad, was it? You won." The suspended moment was broken when a red-faced cowboy put a prod into the bull's hind quarters, making him jump and bolt forward toward the holding pen. Ricki and Mark watched the encounter in amusement and hissed at the cowboy who cast Sarah a disapproving look. The next bull was already out of the chute and in the arena, bucking with might. When the rider left his seat, the bull turned and with head down, bore forward, trying to gore anything that moved. Then he bolted for the opposite end of the arena where he took a lap, pleasing his audience. The cowboy on horseback roped him and led him back toward the outgate and Sarah. Mark and Ricki watched intently. The gate swung open and the bull went through the gate at a full gallop. Sarah was standing about four feet past the gate. The bull came to an abrupt stop next to Sarah, stood still and stared at her. Mark and Ricki started clapping and Ricki shouted, "This is amazing! It's like *Crocodile Dundee*!"

Sarah put her hand out toward the bull and said under her breath, "Good job. Now you can go home and pop a beer." The bull snorted, turned and calmly walked in with the other resting bulls. She glanced at the cowboy. He was looking at her, hands on his hips with a half bewildered, half frightened look on his face. Sarah turned away from his gaze and smiled.

The three of them left the fair and headed toward the cliffs in Mark's truck. It was a clear night and they should be able to see the Milky Way this late in August. As they pulled into the picnic area, they saw their headlights flash across the fence in front of the bathroom building. They got out of the pickup and walked toward the bluff. The field grasses had turned brown, no longer jamming the air with their pungent odors. The sound of waves crashing against the shoreline in the dark below was a sound familiar to them since childhood. Ricki had moved to the town of Sage when she was in fifth grade after her mom died and her dad retired from the Navy. Mark and Sarah were born in Sage and had known each other since kindergarten. Both of their parents were established merchants in Old Town. Mark's dad was an antique dealer while Sarah's parents owned an ice cream parlor two doors from the theater. The teens were now almost seniors in high school and were excited and ambivalent about the next years. They were best friends and were troubled about being catapulted into the world alone, each going their separate way. Their parents had dreams for them to fulfill but sons and daughters have their own dreams, and the three of them were at the difficult age of trying to reconcile the two. They found deep solace in each other, sharing the belief that their parents were never teenagers and only knew established adulthood - *what could parents possibly know of children's dreams?*

They didn't need a flashlight. There was a half-moon mid-sky, preventing a clear glimpse of the Milky Way. Sarah accidently shut her long ash-blonde hair in the car door, triggering a cacophony of laughter that carried east on the strong wind coming off the Pacific. They made their way to the edge and looked down hoping to see something different this night. They had ridden their bikes to this spot for most of their lives and it always looked the same. Sometimes the waves crashed a little harder against the rocks, but other than that, it always looked the same. Tonight, a vessel was anchored offshore, evident by the front running light and the light diffusing from a small galley window. The teens stood silent looking at it. They had never seen a boat so close to their shore at night before.

"What the hell do you suppose that is about?" Mark blurted over the wind. The girls shrugged their shoulders, trying to come up with a plausible explanation.

"Hey, the wind is strong enough tonight. Let's hang it!" Sarah chirped, quickly changing the solemn tone that had begun taking hold of the fun summer night. Sarah's suggestion was a welcome change of tack for Mark, but Ricki's fear of heights was suddenly in her crosshairs again. Ricki reluctantly followed her playmates as they walked toward the cliff where the crashing below was followed by the throw of white lace in the steady moonlight. The onshore wind was strong enough to support their weight as Mark and Sarah leaned over the edge, arms outstretched like eagle's wings, their bodies rigid. Ricki chastised herself as her friends confidently soared, *I will never have enough courage.* She couldn't help fearing what would happen to her friends if the wind had just one hiccup. Her friends would be dead. But she kept silent, longing for the moment when Mark and Sarah became bored with it. She didn't have to wait long. They stopped leaning out when Mark noticed that the boat anchored offshore had moved. It was now near the beach to the north of the bluff, where the Towhee River emptied its guts into the sea and created a churning potato patch on the north side of the confluence. The small vessel was heading for the beach just south of the river. Mark, Sarah and Ricki started for the trail that led through the bushes to the north where they could get a better view. Soon they saw a skiff launch from the boat and head for shore. The landing site was obscured by troll-like shore pines but, through the wind, men's voices could be heard. They watched for a half hour but did not see any additional activity. Mark said he needed to be home by midnight because he had to open the store in the morning.

Ricki and Sarah complained about having to leave and Mark maturely reminded them that Saturdays were big days in the antique business.

For Ricki, Saturday mornings in August were no different than other summer mornings. Senior year would be starting in a few weeks and the lazy mornings of summer would fade into memories again. At least, that is how it has been. As she lay in bed, stretching her long arms and legs, a foreboding apprehension about what life would be like in a year crept in and killed her sense of euphoria. Next summer, a lifetime of adult expectations will have descended upon her head, choking out her spirit. Her dad wanted her to join the Navy and 'make a man of her'. Ricki loved the ocean and couldn't imagine living far from it. But the military? She could only imagine her creative spark being crushed under the power of brutal drill sergeants and men needing to dominate. *No, thank you*, she thought as she lay in bed staring at a wall mural of Hanalei Bay that she painted in her freshman year. If she joined any corps, it would be the Coast Guard. She knew friends that graduated ahead of her that joined The Guard. It was only a two-year commitment and she would probably be stationed on the west coast. She had great respect for the Coast Guard, risking their lives to save others in peril. But she knew that her apprehension of heights was her greatest obstacle - and a formidable one.

The phone rang. It was Sarah, "Ricki, wanna ride our bikes up to the bluffs this morning? I couldn't sleep last night, thinking about that boat. I wanna see if it is still there and hike to Randee Point to see where that skiff landed."

"You're kidding, right?" Ricki's raspy morning voice replied. "We haven't ridden our bikes up there in a very long time! And besides, that was fun last night, but face it, the boat is probably gone and we will never know what that was all about. In 20 years, we will still be saying, 'Remember that night on the bluff when we saw that boat… yada, yada, yada.' It's just childhood fantasy, Sarah."

"C'mon Ricki," Sarah whined, "if the boat is gone, I'll buy you an ice cream at Dip'n'Sip."

"Oh, that's incentive! You give me free ice cream there all the time!" chortled Ricki.

"Okay, I will pay your way to that movie you wanted to see. We could go this afternoon."

"Free ice cream, and a movie?" Ricki paused to contemplate. "Deal!" Ricki swung her legs out of bed and wandered into the bathroom with the remote receiver and looked at her teeth in the mirror. She had forgotten to put her retainer in again last night. Her mom would kill her if her teeth migrated back to that hideous smile.

"Cool, I'll be over around 9:30," Sarah hung up before Ricki had a chance to negotiate time.

The trail leading up to Randee Point was overgrown and rutted. Sarah and Ricki decided to ditch their bikes in the thicket and walk to the top. The morning air was cool yet buzzing with a million insects. A thick bank of fog could be seen offshore. Ricki knew this was a silly idea, coming up to the Point but she was glad she was there, just for the beauty of it. Seldom did she get out in nature this early in the day and she found the nuances of earth's morning rich. As they reached the Point, Ricki focused on the bank of fog veiling the sea's horizon, wondering how long it would be held out there. Sarah noticed the boat anchored close to shore. "It's still there," Sarah said out loud and pointed to the boat anchored at the location where they originally saw it the night before. "I knew it, there is something very *wrong* about this."

Ricki said nothing but looked at the boat, keeping her mind open and remembering that Sarah feels and sees things that others' do not. She had to trust Sarah's gut on this one, "What do we do now?"

"We watch and wait," replied Sarah.

Ricki noted the somberness in Sarah's tone, plopped herself down on the bluff and sucked on a stem of dry grass. Sarah sat next to her and pulled out a pair of binoculars. The boat was a 30-footer fishing boat, the kind that takes tourists out for afternoon excursions. There was no activity on deck. Two unmanned trolling rods were attached to rod holders at the stern, which faced open sea. The skiff, tied to the starboard side of the boat, was barely visible.

"It looks like they are still asleep," handing the binoculars to Ricki. Ricki focused on the boat and then scanned the surrounding sea. She lowered the binoculars and pointed to the north where a rigid inflatable boat with two passengers was motoring its way toward the fishing boat.

"Maybe they're marine biologists, Sarah," Ricki said, handing the binoculars back to Sarah.

"Maybe," Sarah replied slowly with a blatant tone of suspicion.

The friends sat silent waiting for the inflatable boat to reach its destination. Sarah and Ricki both sucked air between their teeth as it tied up portside. Sarah let out a gasp and jerked the binoculars into her lap when she saw a man with a thick black mustache scan the bluff with binoculars, stopping when he saw her looking at him. He pulled up a hand radio and pointed to the girls. She sat frozen as Ricki grabbed the binoculars to see what Sarah had seen. Sarah reached over and knocked the binoculars out of Ricki's hands and barked, "No!" Sarah debated whether to leave or to scan the binoculars across the ocean to make it appear that they were looking for whales. The accelerated activity on both the inflatable and the fishing boat caused her to instinctively start backing away from the edge of the bluff on her elbows, butt and heels. Ricki followed suit. After they clambered down the hill toward the trail that led to where their bikes were stashed, they heard the static of a hand radio. They ran southwest along the base of a rock formation where the vegetation was thick and they could hide. From there they saw two men, standing on the smashed grass where they had previously been sitting, looking feverishly in every direction. Sarah chided Ricki, "Whaddya think now?"

Ricki didn't hesitate, "I think we better do whatever we need to do to get home. My dad will know what to do. This is nuts."

They decided to leave their bikes and hike to the south where they knew of a trail that led across Wilson Creek and up over Thompson Hill to the north. There they would hit Hwy 39 and walk the five miles into town or possibly get a ride from someone they knew. Away from the crashing waves, the morning stillness soothed their nerves and they began to feel confident they were out of danger. They knew the terrain - it was their home turf. Ricki thought about how the morning had begun, lying in bed enjoying a lazy summer day. She mused over how life can randomly throw surprises at you. *Who could've guessed they'd be on this trail evading men with radios and possibly guns?* Again, she started dismissing this as just another adventure that would populate their repertoire of "Remember the time when…" She became vexed once more as she thought about the future. Sarah, walking in front of her, froze when she heard a twig snap. Ricki heard it too which catapulted her from her vaguely vexed state back into an acute state of fear. No other noises followed so they crept silently on a high bank next to a dry creek bed. Ricki tried to not notice how high above the dry creek bed they were walking. Her breathing became labored and dizziness threatened. She kept her eyes on Sarah's shoes walking steadily before her. They crossed the creek bed at a low point and started heading northeast toward Hwy 39. The land that lay between them and Hwy 39 was densely vegetated and uninhabited except by wildlife. The natives tell of a creature that lives in the woods along the northern coast, a tall, hairy, apelike man. Cave drawings had been discovered in the late 1800's depicting a large dark figure standing on a mountain ridge, fists raised. Sarah, Ricki and Mark had made fun of this legend since grade school and would take turns playing 'Squatch' at dusk either in the cemetery or on the beach. Ricki smiled to herself as she thought about those days - summer days like this - where every adventure made time stand still and filled life with a surreal glory. Her father told her she lived in a dream world. He made it sound like it was a bad thing - a mental illness or a personality disorder.

Life was magical to her. Her memories were like melodies, like reflections off still water. And they were always available to her whenever she needed to be comforted or find solace after a disappointment. She could remember her mother's voice comforting her, *"God will command His angels to minister to you, to lift you up with their hands so that you do not dash your foot on a rock."* This saying particularly placated her when her heart was gripped in the fear of falling. Her mother passed away not long before they moved to Sage. Her illness was unexpected and her death swift, leaving Ricki and her dad reeling in disbelief. "So much for looking forward to the golden years," her dad had complained bitterly. Ricki made a choice to be like her mother and not like her father who was a practiced pessimist. Her mom possessed an unshakable joy that was infectious, showing Ricki the silver lining in every situation. *A modern-day Mary Poppins,* Ricki labeled her mom as she followed Sarah through the brush, dependent on her friend's instincts. Without warning, Sarah's fingers jabbed Ricki's chest. She had stopped and jutted her hand behind her to stop Ricki. In front of them lay a black plastic hose stretching from east to west. There were no farmhouses within several miles. The most obvious explanation was that there was a pot farm in the area. Ricki's dad had warned her for years about staying clear of pot growers because they will do whatever they need to do to protect their harvest. Ricki stepped over the hose in front of Sarah with deliberation and headed directly north. Without saying a word, Sarah followed. They marched quickly across a small meadow and into the woods that lined Hwy 39. When they reached the highway, they relaxed and began talking again. "Should we go to the Sheriff?" Sarah asked.

"No, not yet," Ricki answered. "Let's grab Mark and then find my dad. He'll be able to size things up." They had walked on the highway a mile when Mrs. Winkler, a classmate's mom, recognized them and pulled over. Once in the car, they tried to make small talk, explaining how they had been hiking and got lost. Mrs. Winkler dropped them off in town in front of Mark's store.

Mark was carrying an end table across the sidewalk toward an open car trunk when the girls climbed out of Mrs. Winkler's car. His puzzled expression let Ricki and Sarah know that he knew something was up. He handed a receipt to the proud new owner of the mahogany table and turned back towards the entry of the store. At the door, he turned and said, "What's up?"

"When do you get done?" Sarah asked.

"Four."

"Can you come to my house after work? We need to talk to my dad about what we saw last night. Sarah and I went out early this morning to have a look at that boat and we can't be sure, but we think we were just chased across country. Mrs. Winkler stopped and picked us up on Hwy 39 by Beuler's place. Our bikes are still up by the Point."

Mark's jaw went slack momentarily before it started shooting questions.

"Just come to my house after work," Ricki said, "we'll fill in the blanks when my dad gets home."

Don had been helping a buddy rebuild a carburetor for his '57 Chevy all day and was in the shower when his daughter and friend came home. Ricki and Sarah were in the living room watching River Monsters when he moseyed into the kitchen for a beer. They knew he liked this program about unusual river wildlife and would sit down and hang with them if it was on. Fifteen or so minutes after Mark arrived and joined the girls on the couch, Don grabbed the remote from Ricki, punched mute and said, "Okay, what's going on?" The teens exchanged glances as if to say, *how does he know?*

"I know you three Musketeers well enough to know something is up," Don quipped before taking the last gulp of beer.

"Dad?" Ricki began, stalling out.

"Yeah. What's up?"

They began to tell him what had happened the night prior and how Sarah and Ricki had gone out to Randee

Point in the morning. As they described what they saw, how the man on the boat saw Sarah spying with her binoculars, and how quickly the men appeared on the bluff, Don's face became hardened like a gambler's face – a dam holding back a volume of emotion and information.

"Maybe we're just being paranoid, Dad, but something feels wrong - very, very wrong."

Ricki's dad, struggling with temptation to scold his daughter for playing detective, validated the girls' concern about the boat, the binoculars and the hand radios. He went to the kitchen and lifted the receiver off the wall phone.

Mark and Sarah were still sleeping in the living room of Ricki's house Sunday morning when Sheriff Mooney rang the doorbell. He took their statements and left. Sarah asked about retrieving their bikes and were sternly warned by both Mooney and Don to stay away from the bluffs. Mooney said he would have his deputies pick up the bikes when they went out to investigate.

Days went by and nothing else came up about the incident. The bikes were returned to their owners and summer resumed. Sarah's family headed off to Vancouver for their customary late summer vacation, leaving Mark and Ricki to bear boredom. The temptation to go back up to the Point became too strong one evening and they drove up to the bluffs parking area, despite Don's stern stance on 'The Incident' as he called it. The bluffs were a popular spot for viewing sunsets, making their presence non-anomalous. There were several cars dutifully parked, headlights pointed out to sea. Ricki thought it would make a funny picture if the cars had sunglasses on. They walked toward the bluff to get a better panorama and felt relief, mixed with disappointment, that the ocean was devoid of boats. It made Ricki feel insignificant, as though they had merely dreamed up the entire episode. *Silly little children.* Ricki had grown tired of pestering her dad for updates on the Sheriff's investigation. There was no information on the boat, the men or the black irrigation hose. Ricki and Mark sat on the bluff taking in the sunset, solemnly thinking about their final year of high school.

School started up and the cherished memories of her last childhood summer were already getting smaller and smaller in Ricki's rearview mirror. French class was predictable with more of the same instructor and more of the same students. "Four years of a foreign language will be a nice bonus when you are in the Navy," her dad had said. She knew that she didn't want to join the Navy but understood that something adventurous like that was probably in the cards. She just didn't know what that was yet. She loved the ocean and because she was good at sleuthing - thanks to her best friend, Sarah - she was considering exploration with National Geographic or the National Oceanic and Atmospheric Administration (NOAA). She just didn't know how to get in position for that sort of thing. A meeting with a school counselor was coming up the week before Thanksgiving and she was hoping to map out a plan. She was apprehensive to tell any of these alternative career paths to her father for fear of crushing him. After losing Mom, he was bent on making sure Ricki had a secure future. She didn't want to disappoint.

1 Dust in the Wind ⊷

Mike rolled on the ground to avoid flying fragments. He knew he was burned. He could smell burnt hair. The sound of shattering glass was nearly drowned out by the roar of the blast. There was ringing in his ears. All thoughts of his own welfare faded as he remembered the moments before when he waved good-bye to Gwynn. He told her to be sure to call as soon as she got back to New York. He knew there would be no call. As the thought sunk in, it reverberated down his throat to his chest, where heavy air clung to wavering pillars of pain. The earth beneath him fell away to blackness and the sirens he heard merged with the darkness before fading into oblivion. *Gwynn!*

The Agent patiently waited at the foot of Mike's bed, looking over his weekly planner. Mike looked around the hospital room without moving so that the Agent wouldn't notice he had awoken. He registered pain in several parts of his body but couldn't tell exactly which parts those were. A cough rose in his throat and he strained to restrain it, until the rising air stung its way into the antiseptic air. Agent McElroy looked up from his planner. "I see you've finally come around, mate. You've been napping for a while now. Mr. Hadler, you are in the intensive care unit at Mount Zion. I have some questions I need to ask you about the explosion. Do you remember the explosion?"

Instantly, the sight of Gwynn standing at the gate waving her hand came crashing through the sweet sublime of morphine. "Gwynn!" The I.V. nearly dislodged as Mike sat up. "What happened? What day is it? The passengers?"

A galaxy of questions swirled around in his head making him lose a grip on the bed rail. When his head landed on the pillow, he felt the ceiling crash down on him. The nurse came in waving disdain towards Agent McElroy. She checked Mike's intravenous needle to make sure no infiltration had occurred and adjusted the morphine dosage. "You need to rest Mr. Hadler. You've sustained several lacerations on your arms and legs and second degree burns on your neck and hands," she said with gentle authority.

"I ...need to know ..." Mike fumbled for words.

"Mr. Hadler, do you remember what happened?" the nurse continued.

"An explosion at the terminal, the plane...", the horror of Gwynn being dead seized him again. "The passengers ... are there any survivors? My fiancée? Someone please tell me!"

"Mr. Hadler, there are no survivors. I'm sorry," the Agent replied flatly.

The Agent's words hung in the air as Mike stared into his stoic face. This passing moment would change his life forever as he crossed over the bridge between yesterday's expectations and tomorrow's fallen reality. He had known and loved Gwynn almost half his life. He brought his untethered hand up to his face and covered his eyes where tears were welling. Agent McElroy waited patiently before continuing his inquiry.

"Terrorists?" Mike's voice cracked mid-syllable.

"Yes, we believe so. Mr. Hadler, I am sorry. I need to ask you some questions."

"Do you know who?"

"It's too early yet. Now, Mr. Hadler, did you see anything unusual about any of the passengers boarding the plane? And how was it that you were at the Gate? You didn't have a boarding pass. I checked all airlines." The agent was working Mike. Mike tried to remember Gate 16 where he waited with Gwynn for the boarding call. He had observed a mother accompanying a pubescent boy - her son he assumed. He recalled a family of seven anxiously waiting for their vacation to see the Statue of Liberty. There was a colicky salesman who annoyingly yammered loudly on his cell phone for the entire duration of the wait. And a youngish-looking guy with short haphazard dreadlocks, who dozed off and on, drowsily awaiting his fight. Agent McElroy penciled into his notebook the description of these last two characters and asked if there were any other characters that stood out in his mind. Mike added, "A young woman, short blonde hair. No, some was pink. Lots of studs, ears, nose, chin. She chewed gum fast."

"How old?" McElroy prompted.

"Young. 18, 19, 20 - hard to say. Lots of eye make-up," Mike replied. When he exhausted his memory, the agent admonished him for using his reporter pass to gain entrance to the terminal gates and then handed him an FBI card telling him to call if he remembered anything else.

Mike was released from Mount Zion five days after the explosion. Gwynn's sister and only surviving relative, Carolyn, drove from Phoenix to arrange for Gwynn's memorial service. After the service, Mike and Carolyn spent the evening in Carlisle's Pub on Green Street, crying and laughing over memories of Gwynn. They lamented because they couldn't spread Gwynn's ashes over Pyramid Peak in the Sierra Nevada Mountains as she requested one time after drinking too much champagne. That was the same trip when she requested room service to the wrong room while staying at the Corsico Hotel in San Diego. She had asked for a hair dryer that wasn't broken, extra blankets and two extra pillows. The woman in the room across the hall waved the room service man away, his arms overflowing with the items Gwynn requested. Gwynn only discovered the mistake when Carolyn had returned from the beach claiming she saw a very confused bellman loaded up like a jackass being sworn at by a woman in room 205.

The *Inquisitor* wasn't pressing Mike to return to work soon. Fortunately, he had several weeks of sick leave and vacation. However, he didn't know what to do with himself and wondered if going back to work wouldn't have been the best thing for him. He took down all the pictures of Gwynn and put her collection of colognes in a drawer, where on occasion, he would take one out and smell it.

The news was calling it a terrorist bombing carried out by a watchdog environmental group calling themselves Neptune. Neptune promoted the cessation of ocean exploration for petroleum, gas and minerals. Their web site that Mike pulled up said that oceans are the well spring of our planet, and as the dominant species on the planet, man must protect and serve the oceans - no matter the cost. Mike didn't understand how murderers could have a web site and not be arrested. It was last updated eight months ago. Certainly, the FBI was aware of it. He found Agent McElroy's card and rang him up. He punched in the extension number and after listening to McElroy's voicemail greeting, left a call-back number. He thought, *it could be days with these government guys.* He would give the feds a couple weeks to see what they uncover before he spent time sleuthing. Sniffing out a story and ferreting out the truth was an integral part of his nature. He was a newspaper reporter, and news reporters were like bloodhounds always on a hunt. He was a staff writer for the Investigation Section of the *San Francisco Inquisitor*, now going on his eighth year. Gwynn had wanted him to scale back into a more socially-oriented form of journalism, instead of busting his butt all the time competing with super-aggressive and hungry upshots who would sell their own mother to get a story. A less demanding position would be more conducive for continuing their long-distance relationship, at least until she moved out to California.

He called his boss again. Fogerty told him to take the time he needed before coming back to work. He also told him his job would be there for him when he was ready. Mike hung up and reflected how fortunate he was to work for a man like Jeff Fogerty. He called the *Inquisitor* again but this time dialed Sarah's extension. Sarah was a co-worker whose work and style he had admired since she began working at the paper six years ago. They worked on several stories together and had developed a strong comradery. She would claim he mentored her, but Mike did not agree. Sarah had bloodhound in her and that is what makes or breaks a journalist.

"Hey, Sarah."

"Mike? Great to hear from you! I've missed you here. When do you think you'll get bored and come back to work?"

"Well, it's good to know somebody misses me! Fogerty keeps telling me to take as much time as I need. He is starting to worry me a little bit."

"Oh, shhh. You know he loves the heck out of you. You're his pet. Mike, I am so sorry about Gwynn. I don't know what to say. You got my card? I saw you at the memorial, but you were busy with family. When will you get bored and come back to work?" she repeated the question.

"Not for a while. I might take a drive to Palm Springs and clear my head out a little. I'm not sure who I am anymore. But I have a favor to ask. You are good with the web. How would you go about finding the location of a someone or group with a web page? How would you track it?"

Sarah was quiet for a moment noting to herself that it was 2011, post 911, and Mike should already know the answers to questions regarding online investigations. "You would need to go to the dark web - find internet provider numbers and find the location of the server that supports the home page. Who do you want to track?"

Mike continued, "The group, Neptune, is supposedly claiming responsibility for the explosion that killed Gwynn. They have a web site. It hasn't been updated recently. Someone has to be responsible for payment to the server provider, right?"

"Yes. However, it is easier and easier these days to create alias domains and set up offshore accounts. Hackers do it all the time. So do terrorists. There is nothing tying you to a physical domicile. That's why it's called the ethernet. As long as the internet service provider gets paid, what do they care where the money is coming from? Achieving anonymity has become child's play. The CIA, Homeland Security, et cetera, et cetera, have amped up resources for hunting down terrorists and other ghouls of the net. Espionage and corporate spying has gone where no man has gone before. Did you say this group is international?"

"Yes, international, Scotty," he replied coyly. "Well, I'll wait to see what the FBI turns up. But, if they're snails in finding those who are responsible for Gwynn's death, I will personally go after them."

"Mike, you aren't going to become obsessed with this, are you? Go off on your own maniacal investigation and get yourself killed or make yourself looney? Why don't you think about coming back to the office? At least come to our Christmas party. Let those who are trained and paid take the risks."

"Risks are part of our business, Sarah. And besides, do you really think I can just let this go? Just forget about it and get on with my life? I keep thinking – regretting - that we never tied the knot. Never had kids. Never had the house with a swing set in the backyard. And a dog. We couldn't decide on what breed of dog. We couldn't debate what kind of kid we would have, but we certainly could debate what kind of dog." Mike realized he was going down an emotional rabbit hole and backed out, "I thought we still had lots of time."

"Just don't do anything stupid, Mike."

"I'm not. I am going to take a long drive and let the dust in my head settle. Then I will figure out something. Don't worry. It was good to hear your voice. Work hard, Sarah."

The last comment calmed Sarah's concern that Mike would be forever crippled by the tragic event. She would hate to see one of the most wonderful people she knew get screwed up. "Feel free to call me," she said with genuine gentleness.

"Okie-dokie," Mike pushed the speaker button to hang up. He had every intention of sleeping through Christmas.

He put his car into reverse and backed-up far enough to swing out of his parking place. Grove St. was nearly devoid of traffic so early on a Sunday morning. The whole city seemed asleep still even though it was already 8:30. Everyone was either recuperating from the previous week's insane pace, from their Saturday night adventures, or both. Underneath the numbness, he was excited about his trip. He knew the hours behind the wheel would afford him plenty of time to reflect on Gwynn, the loss, the future, his revenge, justice.

Once past the Carquinez Bridge, he put his Jetta on cruise control and let himself relax and begin the process of letting his mind freewheel and think some things through. He began thinking about how Gwynn had been the best part of his life for more than half of his life. Part of the time driving, he believed she was still alive, working in New York. The other half of the time, he remembered her waving good-bye at the gate, smiling that captivating smile, her red hair swinging like a veil of polished copper as she turned to board the plane. That's when the freight train of grief would crash in on him, leaving him doubled over, wondering how he would make it through the next 20 minutes. He needed this road trip to give himself liberty to feel, think, yell, cry, hate, love, kill. In Roseville, he pulled off the freeway into a gas station and sobbed until he fell asleep. When he woke up it was nearly noon.

Reno was dazzling at night and he wove his way through the various casinos on the street rather than use the interconnecting walkways that link them into one huge playground. He had booked a room at the Silver Legacy and went for a swim before dinner. He managed 24 laps before a gaggle of raucous children came to the pool and splattered all around him, yelling "*Marco? Polo!*" The night he met Gwynn at his best friend's cousin's pool party in Branson they had played *Marco Polo*. She was on summer vacation in Branson with her mother. He was 17 then. As the memory seized him, he muttered, "Damn! I can't get away from it, and I can't live with it!" The children in the pool froze and, with trepidation, slowly backed away from the nefarious stranger. He got out of the pool and retreated to his room where he drank a half a bottle of Zinfandel and fell asleep. He got out of bed four days later.

2 Transposed ⋘

When she arrived at the airport, Monica noted the dread with which she gathered her bag and headed out to hail a taxi. She felt a bit like Bill Murray in the movie *Ground Hog Day*. Year after year she went to the same meeting. And year after year she came home only a little bit more informed than she was before she went. Why would 2012 be any different? What new information gained from the twentieth Flora and Fauna Genome Conference could reignite a fire in her long-dead enthusiasm for research. Biotech and pharmaceutical companies were at full gallop now in the field of biotech research, creating consortium monopolies and an employment labyrinth for postdocs which amounted to not much more than a glorified labor pool. The FFG Conference was an annual event where professors could showcase their prodigies and programs. State and government research facilities were no longer the champions in crop research, advancing the science for the good of humanity. Now research was driven by the market, with patents and biotech startup shareholders most highly sought. She had thought about leaving government work and joining one of these cutting-edge corporations, but in her gut she had adverse feelings about the newly evolving social order of science.

San Diego seemed warmer than it had in the last three Januarys. If the weather was conducive, maybe she would make time for a short trip to Coronado Beach or a visit to the zoo. The flora at the San Diego Zoo always pleased her more than the fauna. Monica was a northern California girl who loved summer. By mid-winter, she craved the warm radiation of the SoCal sun on her back. It was her guess that most of the people who came to the FFG conference did so only because being in San Diego in January was like being in the tropics compared to the harsh winters in Baltimore, Fort Collins or Madison.

The taxi driver lifted her bag from the trunk and deposited it at the front door of the hotel, wrote her a receipt and helped his next fare into the back seat of his car. Monica carefully stuck the receipt into a pocket of her wallet. A gaggle of colleagues were in the lobby of the hotel. Some were checking in and others were gathering for happy hour and long discussions about their newest ideas. Dwayne saw Monica and hollered to her, "Hey,

Monica, would you like to join us for dinner? We are heading over to the Gas Lamp District."

"Oh, that sounds great! But I need to check into my room and get settled. You guys go on. I'll catch up with you another night."

Monica would have enjoyed taking the train to the Gas Lamp District. It was something she looked forward to each year. But she needed to first check-in for the conference and put up her poster. Then she could play. She was happy she didn't need to present a paper this year. She had done so last year entitled *Post-transcriptional Modification of Ubiquitin in Tomato*. This year she would be free of the intense pressure, however, at the expense of being invisible. When a researcher gave a talk, people sought out the speaker to discuss nuances of the experiment, thus, making the conference more interesting and productive. Since publishable results were usually years away, the attention from peers felt like a burst of wind in a luffing sail.

Monica let a bellman transport her and her baggage to her room on an electric cart. She had asked for a Garden room near the east wall of the grounds. It was a hike from her room to the Conference Center, but it was always welcome in the early morning or after a long afternoon of listening to talks in a dim room, trying like heck not to head bob. There was a pub on the grounds nearby where conference-goers networked after hours, drinking copious amounts of rum like pirates and spilling their guts about where the treasured booty called 'funding' could be found.

After dusk, with her poster tucked under her arm, she walked over to the conference center hoping to find somebody she knew on the way. She abhorred wandering around aimlessly looking for people to network with, so she was happy she had a purpose. She noted clusters of people walking and laughing, but none of them looked familiar. She found the conference registration station, signed in, and received her packet which consisted of a silk-screened tote-bag, a program, a banquet ticket, a nametag and the perfunctory sponsored swag (a monitor brush and a small flash light with a double helix painted on the side). Instead of putting her nametag on her jacket, she put it inside the program in the bag. As she turned to enter the poster area, Pederik Roogam and Dana Oiygen came up the stairs and invited Monica to have a late dinner with them and several others at a nearby mall. They agreed to meet at the FFG registration station at 7:45 and they exchanged room numbers for future reference.

Monica had 45 minutes to slap up her poster, go back to her room to drop off the tube and tote-bag and get her backpack. She was assigned poster number 134. When she found board 134, it was occupied by a poster regarding the expression of antifreeze protein in *Mus musculus* by someone from UC San Diego. There were already posters in 133 and 136, and the only one left vacant was 135. She thought about moving the poster from 134 into the adjacent vacant one. And then she thought about just switching the numbers. She read the poster to see if she knew the researcher that took her spot, but she didn't recognize any of the author names, or the work. She decided to let it go and just use board 135. She thought, *People will figure out the simple transposition as they walk through the poster room.* She finished putting her poster up and stood back to admire it. She had worked hard on the experiment and thought she had made great headway in characterizing the role ubiquitin plays in cyclin degradation and apoptosis. *It was good work*, she thought as two men briskly walked past her, barely glancing at her. When they got to the end of the aisle, they stopped to commiserate over something.

She plucked up her plastic poster tube and registration material and started back to her room. As she passed the first parking lot, she heard people splashing and laughing in the nearby pool. A car edged its way behind her and as she moved over to the side of the way, it pulled up alongside to pass. At that moment she felt a hand on her mouth and her arm being pulled up tight behind her back. The pain in her shoulder made her yelp and drop her belongings. Someone's knee was pushing into her lower back as the car's back door opened and she was shoved inside. Immediately, darkness came as something was pulled over her head and a string was tied around her neck. Anger rose in her throat and obscenities, sharpened by fear, slashed like a sword from her mouth. Her hands came up wildly in response to the string around her neck and then they were apprehended and cuffed behind her back. She kicked against the door and window, squealing like a wild animal and then all was still.

3 World on Fire ◄

Lydia leaned forward in her chair, "I don't see how making Shara apologize to that moron is appropriate. He provoked her! I would've scratched his face too. I want to talk to his parents. May I please have their phone number?"

"Well, the school is not allowed to give out student's phone numbers Mrs. Tankersley," the rotund man said, "but, I'll see if I can arrange a meeting."

"Thank you, Mr. Halloway. I would appreciate that."

Lydia got up to leave and the hem of her skirt got caught on the chair's arm. She tugged on it and there was a small tearing sound. More than slightly irritated, she turned savagely on Mr. Halloway,"That boy touches Shara again I'll kill 'm!"

The principal, instantly losing respect for Lydia, ignored the outburst and simply returned his attention to the papers on his desk. Mothers bored him. His attempt to hide that fact became apparent when conversations turned sour. Lydia drove the back-way home, hoping it would give her time to understand what made her lose control. It was often that way with her. She could be composed, sophisticated, well-mannered, effective and then whammo! the air would turn crimson and balls of whirling fire would swarm within, and shortly thereafter, find release through her mouth. There would be no warning and she was always ashamed afterwards. Her wrath seemed to be free-wheeling, always searching for a target. This time it came forth to defend her beloved daughter. At breakfast that morning, however, it roared out at her defenseless daughter. Shara had cried, wondering what she had done to make her mother so upset with her. She never considered that it was not about her at all. Lydia hated herself for it and wanted to change. Dr. Karrington had been beneficial in helping her discover the underlying causes of her free-floating anxiety. But knowing it and actually changing it were two different things. There was no way to bring closure to the wound that had festered inside her all these years. Sometimes she wondered if her husband had been right in suggesting that she be hospitalized. Luckily the judge had seen this antic as merely a strategy to gain sole custody of Shara. He had made it sound like she walked the house nightly with a butcher knife looking for intruders. Carl wasn't afraid to use any strategy to get what he wanted. She always thought he would make a good prosecutor. He could dig dirt out of an angel's fingernail if he wanted an indictment bad enough. Their marriage of five years ended in a nasty court battle in which joint custody was granted. Shara spent long weekends and some holidays with her father in Las Vegas. Otherwise she lived with Lydia in San Diego and frequently visited Carl's recently widowed mother.

Lydia held a good position at University of California San Diego. She headed up research on antifreeze protein (AFP) analogs in mice. AFPs were first found in flounder and then in other marine life. They provided the ability to survive extremely cold environments by preventing the formation of ice crystals in cytoplasm. More recently they had been discovered in beetles and other terrestrial species. She had one postdoc and several graduate students trying to determine the role ATFs played in terrestrial mammals. The postdoc was exhibiting a poster at the upcoming *Flora and Fauna Genome XX Conference* at the Shine and Explore Conference Center in the Mission Valley neighborhood. This year, she was happy to be able to send someone else to present her research. She had attended for the last six years and gave a talk at the Abiotic Workshop last year and the year before that. She had arranged to meet with some colleagues for dinner at Fio's Tuesday night but other than that, she was staying away from the conference and concentrating on her work. She missed her peers from Memorial University and looked forward each year when they made the annual trek to San Diego. They always brought a bit of home with them and, of course, were faithfully interested in her advances in AFP research. She had followed her father's passion for science even though she did not have direct exposure to it. Her father had not been a part of her life since she was very young and, after her mother died, she was raised by his sister in Halifax, Nova Scotia. He was assumed dead but there had never been any confirmation of that. She entered Arctic research at Memorial University after high school and remained there for graduate school. She took her first postdoc appointment in British Columbia where she met Carl. He was a patent lawyer for the University. Her principal investigator was engaged in marketing novel promoter sequences. He asked her to lunch one day and things snowballed from there. A year and a half later they were married with a child on the way. Shara was born in 2005 and when she was one year old, they moved from British Columbia to southern California where Carl started his own firm and Lydia took a position at the University of California, San Diego. Her father had been employed by UC San Diego back in the late fifties. Even though she never connected herself to the man, she was fairly certain that his reputation gave her a leg up in landing the job.

4 Jokes and Genes

Her eyes were open, but she couldn't see. Her mind skittered in circles trying to discern where she was and what time it was, and then Monica remembered she was at a conference. She reassured herself all was well by asserting that she always gets disorientated the first night at a motel. However, images of her screaming and lashing at unknown enemies streaked through her head like flashes of lightning low on the horizon. Her head hurt. Did she get drunk with Pederik and Dana? Sluggishly, she raised her left hand to her face and the right hand followed. Her hands were bound and a soft cloth covered her face. She tried to pull the cloth down, thinking it was a slip that fell out of her suitcase onto the bed. It wouldn't come off. She sat up and discovered that the cloth was a bag over her head. Horror seized her as the images of being shoved into a car replayed in her mind, *oh God! It was real. No! Can't be!* She attempted to roll off the bed, but her feet were restrained. She squinted into the darkness to make out her surroundings but could see very little. It was comfortably warm and smelled like it had recently been vacuumed. She could hear a faucet dripping in the next room. The bed was comfortable with a buttress of pillows at the headboard. There were short footboard posts to which her feet were strapped with some sort of cuff. *This can't be really happening to me*, she chanted to herself.

Through the soft cloth she could see a vertical slit of light to her right. She guessed it was daylight through thick drapes. Another hint of light escaped under a closed door that was on the opposite side of the bed and her thoughts ran wild. *Who would want me? I am nobody. Why are they doing this to me?* She heard footsteps outside the room and an exchange of low voices. Soon the light under the door was interrupted with dark shadows. The door's latch turned and the room suddenly was cast in light. The silhouette in the door offered no information except that it was male, about 5 foot 8 inches tall, thin.

"I see you have woken refreshed, Ms. Lomax. We got a little rough with you last night, or more accurately, you got rough with us. One of my colleagues, Grady, suffered a broken thumb due to your tenacious kicking. If you have a headache, it is because we used chloroform on you."

"What do you want? Why are you doing this to me? I have nothing you could possibly want!" She felt herself beginning to fall into the helplessness that often threatened her courage. She fought back the tears and let the scientist in her prevail, "What do you want?"

"Ms. Lomax, you have knowledge that we want."

Monica, stunned, scanned her mind, her career, her life and could not find anything that could be valuable to someone else. And her name was not Lomax. Sure, her work was important but how could ubiquitin be important to anyone. Then she thought about the airport - had someone stuck something in her bag? Her mind jumped to Will Smith in the movie *Enemy of the State*.

"I don't know what I have that you want, but you can have all my luggage. I'll give you my hotel key and you can just go get it. I'll never speak of this."

The suave man chuckled, closed the door and moved toward her. As he snipped the plastic zip-tie keeping the bag on her head, he replied, "Ms. Lomax, we want knowledge, not your possessions." His thick French accent made his voice sound affectionate, almost kind. But his sinister chuckle made her neck hairs stand on end. "Why do you keep calling me Ms. Lomax? My name is Linden. Monica Linden. And I know nothing that would be interesting to anyone except some pathetic seed company looking to lose stock!" She was beginning to feel indignant and her smartass words made the French thug move stealthily towards her. Sitting on the edge of the bed next to her, he brushed his hand against her limp hair. She bolted as far as she could away from him. Her ankles burned from the straps.

"Madam, would you like for your hands and feet untied so you could run further from me? You hurt my feelings," he mocked her.

His caring tone and cruel chuckle slammed against each other, causing her to break out in a sweat. She sensed the dangerous web he was spinning for her. She decided to accept no kindness from him.

"No, thank you. I'll wait until your boss shows up."

The French thug rose to his feet, grunted and left the room, bleeding from his libido. Monica felt chilled as the door closed and darkness filled the room again. She pulled some blankets over herself and felt her sense of helplessness seep out through tears. Her smart mouth! It always got her in trouble - in high school and college. One time at UC Berkeley, she had a professor who thought the world of himself. He taught dendrology and habitually embarrassed students for no apparent reason and with no mercy. She had come into lecture five minutes late because she needed to borrow money for parking. Dr. Lucas had already started lecturing, when he saw Monica winding her way to a seat. In a flat monotone voice, he said, "Well, Ms. Linden, I suppose you already know how to tell a female from a male yew tree. Thus, you feel it is completely unnecessary to arrive in time for the beginning of today's lecture." All 260 heads turned her way, and with redness creeping up the skin of her throat, she calmly replied, "Well, yes Sir, I do." Her mind scrambled for something clever to say next. So much was at stake! All eyes were on her. Dr. Lucas raised his head with an arrogant and triumphant expression, his trap having been set. "Well, it's quite easy you see, Dr. Lucas. You simply pull down their genes and look." The auditorium roared with laughter and Monica felt an immense sense of pleasure for outwitting the bastard that had so cruelly antagonized the entire class all semester. She basked in the light of her classmates' admiration, until she felt it shadowed by a growing tower of wrath emanating from the enraged man at the chalkboard. The lecture hall eventually fell silent and with a deadly gaze directed at Monica, he pensively snapped his chalk in half and left the hall. The next day she was removed from his class roster.

If her feet were free, maybe she could find a way to escape. *Damn it, why had she been so stupid?* She cried and then she slept. When she woke up, she had to pee fiercely. She hollered, "Hey! I gotta go pee! Somebody?" There was no response. She yelled two more times for attention, but there was no response. She'd seen stories on the news or in movies where a hostage wasn't allowed the decency of civilized toiletry and often wondered what that would be like. Now she knew. She thought of how the Nazis crammed thousands of Jewish men, women and children into freight cars without ventilation or amenities for hours, days. *Corrie Ten Boom.* Well, it's only pee she thought. She managed to pull down her pants and maneuvered her torso until her butt was over the side of the bed and started to empty her bladder. Before she was finished, she heard footsteps outside her room. She yanked her pants up and flopped herself back onto the bed. Embarrassment and anger engulfed her. *Keep your cool* she told herself. *Be charming.*

"You were yelling, Mademoiselle?" It was Frenchie again.

"Yes, I needed to go - I need to use the bathroom."

"Okay, I will ask *The Boss*" he sneered at her, reminding her of her recent insult. He pulled a phone from his pocket and spoke into it. "Mr. Tilden, Ms. Lomax needs to use the facilities. Shall I let her?" There was a pause and then Frenchie said, "Okay, sure."

"Mademoiselle, you can use the bathroom." As he walked around the side of the bed, his shoes made a sucking sound on the carpet. Monica saw, in the dim light, a sinister grin appeared on Frenchie's face. "Ah

Mademoiselle, but I can see you have already used the bathroom." His tone was teasing and affectionate yet carried a disturbing steel edge.

"Yeah, but I didn't get to finish." Monica wanted to rip his throat out for humiliating her. Calming herself she mustered up charm, "I still need to go".

He loosened the cuffs that secured her hands and feet, "Yes, Mademoiselle, you will use the bathroom and then you will see *The Boss*." A vacuous grin consumed his face, revealing a generous gap between his front teeth. He led her to a door that concealed a bathroom and flicked on the light. The bright light accosted her vision and her arm went up involuntarily to provide shade. Her head hurt.

He closed the door and she locked it. She pulled down her pants and sat on the toilet, looking around for something that might help her escape. First thing she looked for was a window. There wasn't one. There were your basic towels, floor rugs, shower curtain, plus a vanity with some drawers and a wicker clothes hamper. She got up and explored the vanity drawers and the clothes hamper. She found nothing obviously useful. There were towels and face cloths, soap, cotton swabs, toothpaste and three new toothbrushes. She flushed the toilet and stood in front of the mirror. She looked wretched. Her eyes were sunk in deep sockets making her look 44 instead of 34. Her warm brown hair hung limp in tangled mats. She ran her fingers through it to smooth it out. She brushed her teeth. She needed all the time she could get. She stuck a few cotton swabs in her pockets. When she was done brushing her teeth, she washed her face and then rubbed the damp washcloth on her neck, armpits and genital area where pee had dried. She searched the room for anything that might help her.

"Mademoiselle?"

"I'm washing up. Give a girl a break!" she blurted, panic narrowing her vision.

Frenchie smiled, admiring women in general. Before she turned off the faucet, for an unknown reason, she lifted the floor rug that was in front of the vanity. She noticed a large pink safety pin and shoved it into her back pocket. Frenchie knocked loudly on the door, "Mademoiselle or no, you are trying my patience. Do not forget, I have a key. I can come in when I like."

Realizing her time was up, Monica straightened the floor rug and walked to the door. "Alright-already! I'm finished." She opened the door and there was Frenchie, smiling, ready to escort her like his date to a banquet. Out of the room and into a long hall, her brain recorded everything she observed: *Left down a corridor and left down another. Dark green carpet, two-toned painted walls with a strip of border near the ceiling. Pictures of seascapes with gaudy frames metering the long walls.* It reminded her of the decor she had seen at a Heldon Hotel on the Gulf Coast once. When they got in the elevator, Frenchie put a pair of dark sunglasses on her. She could not see through them. Monica tried to compose herself, masking her fear. She tried to calculate how much fear to let through her veneer of insolence. Or was it the other way around? The elevator stopped a couple floors down. They turned right, away from the sound of children splashing in a pool. The smell of chlorine filled her nostrils and then faded as they walked. They stopped abruptly and still holding Monica's arm, Frenchie straightened his sport jacket before knocking on a door. When it opened, he roughly pushed Monica forward. The room smelled of cigar. The dark glasses were removed from her face and the cigar smoke immediately started irritating her eyes. Two men sat on a large desk in front of a bay window facing a lake and three men and a woman stood near the right wall behind two large U-backed chairs. All but the woman were dressed like they worked the financial district - well-fitting suits and short groomed hair. The super-fit Latino woman, wearing a camo tank top, stood with her hand on the handle of a pistol like she was waiting for a shootout. Frenchie pulled Monica across the room to a chair placed in front and left of the desk. One of the men sitting halfway on the desk had stood to his feet and walked around to the chair behind the desk. "Please, sit down

Miss Lomax." Monica frowned, her head throbbing and her breath short.

"Miss Lomax, we regret putting you through the uncomfortable side effects of chloroform, but you really put up quite a noisy fight I hear. I hope your accommodations were comfortable."

Monica listened intently, deciding to find out as much as she could from them before opening her mouth and disclosing any information about herself. The man went on, "You see, Miss Lomax, we need your expertise in a certain subject matter. We have followed your work and find it very interesting." Monica bit her tongue as she felt an indignant outburst rising in her throat. She wanted to snap, *"Then you could've looked me up at my poster, or contacted me by email, you ignorant red-assed baboon!"* Instead, she kept eye contact with the man who spoke. She tried to ascertain the hierarchy of power in the room. Obviously, the man speaking ranked high, but wasn't necessarily the highest. She eyed the other man leaning against the desk. They were close in age and they dressed similar. *Brothers maybe.* The others, including Frenchie, sat or stood soundlessly watching.

"We are businessmen, Miss Lomax, and would like to make you an offer. We have a laboratory that is very well equipped with all the supplies and reagents you need to continue your research on thermal hysteresis. You would be rewarded robustly." He paused before continuing, "Well?"

Now Monica had the picture, *Thermal hysteresis! The poster that took her poster board was on antifreeze proteins and thermal hysteresis! In what species? She couldn't remember. That's who Lomax is - the author of the poster in her slot! They wouldn't let her go if they knew they had the wrong person, would they? If they knew she wasn't Lomax? What should she do? Could she fake it? Bluff them? Probably for a while, but eventually they would find out. Dammit, businessmen buy innovations not steal them!* She was caught up in an internal rage and when she looked up, they were staring at her. She realized they were waiting for a response to their question about employment.

"Mr. … uh?" she stammered, forgetting what Frenchie had called him.

"To you, Mr. Yes will suffice".

She growled internally, "Yes, well Mr. Yes, most businessmen arrange to buy and patent innovations, not kidnap them." She felt righteous in her response.

The two men at the desk exchanged glances. A smile came over the face of the man speaking to her. "I guess you can say we are progressive businessmen." The room broke into laughter and Mr. Yes lit a cigar. Monica began to feel overwhelmingly vulnerable, her cloak of bravado beginning to vacillate between rage and panic.

"Do you know why I am called Mr. Yes, Miss Lomax?" Mr. Yes spoke with a passively pensive face.

Monica looked at him for his answer, bracing herself against it.

"Because everyone I know always replies with 'yes'. Isn't that right, Charlie? Isn't that right Jean-Marc?" The man leaning on the desk and Frenchie chimed at the same time, "Yes. Absolutely. Yes." Laughter made its heavy footprint in the air again. They were breaking her down. They were not new at this and she was beginning to understand that she may never get out of this alive. Real fear set in and it was obvious to her kidnappers.

"I can see that you understand the situation that you find yourself in, Miss Lomax. And I would advise you to not resist our requests." He put down his barely-smoked cigar, sat down and folded his hands in front of him on the desk. His receding hairline left shiny patches of scalp that reflected the light from the window. "That's all for now. Jean-Marc, take her back to her room and bring her a good meal."

Back in her room, with drapes pulled and the door locked, she was free to move about. She opened the drapes to explore prospects of escape. The room was three floors up. The window was key-locked and looked over a courtyard, richly landscaped with tropical flora, complete with a kidney-shaped swimming pool, lounge chairs, glass tables, umbrellas and a palapa-covered bar. There was a woman laying on a chaise lounge, reading what looked like a journal reprint. Monica moved around the room examining furniture drawers. All she found was a dated telephone directory of Palm Springs, CA and a *Gideon's Bible*, which she thought was some kind of cruel joke. Not only did it strike her odd that her captives would be so kind as to provide their kidnap victims with the comfort of a Bible, but she didn't believe in God. Nor did any colleagues. In early adolescence, she had abandoned any interest in a greater, benevolent Being. Her father was a truck driver, seldom at home. Her mother, raised Catholic, went to church regularly, holding to the ways taught to her by her father. In the primary grades, Monica attended catechism at her mother and grandfather's insistence. Holy Communion at age seven was a special event in her life that made her feel like she totally belonged to God, that he cared for her like no one else. She prayed every night for five years that her father would stop driving truck and be home more often. Every time he came home, he felt more distant than the time before. Monica grew older, which seemed to further estrange her father. On his arrival she no longer felt she could lunge into his arms for him to throw her up in the air and kiss both cheeks while lowering *"his Princess"* to the floor. Or play leg-launch as he drank coffee at the kitchen table telling of highway adventures between Salt Lake City and Redding, where they lived. One day when she was 11, he stopped coming home. He called his wife and told her that he didn't feel comfortable there anymore and that he found happiness with someone else. He asked for a divorce. From Monica's point of view, God, the Benevolent and Powerful Being that was supposed to care for little children, answered the exact opposite of her faithful prayers. He betrayed her. Her mother spent most nights for the next ten months curled up in a ball watching TV. Eventually, she got a job at the supermarket bagging groceries and when she wasn't working, she was attending Mass. Monica went to summer school every year because her mother couldn't afford summer camp. There she discovered that she loved the life sciences. She had her first male teacher in the summer between 7th and 8th grade. He taught Biology. She learned about dividing cells, DNA replication and transcription, about the cellular machinery that turned a messenger RNA molecule into a protein, how life began in a primordial soup from a single cell, and from these cells all forms of life differentiated. The begats of this system made much more sense to her than the begats of the Bible. So, that was the summer she stopped believing in God - even a negligent God. Her mother, to this day, often calls her, begging her to listen to a tape by so-and-so or to a song that 'lifts Jesus higher'.

"Monica, you need to start going to Mass again," she would whine. Monica would kindly decline, finding some excuse why she needed to get off the phone. She encouraged her mom to call her sister. Tanya still believed in God.

She pulled the Bible out of the drawer and looked at the inside of the cover. Stamped there was *Gideon's Light, Chapter 12, New Orleans, LA*. She wondered if the book came with the furniture from some motel these businessmen bought - or stole - in New Orleans. She dropped the Bible on the nightstand and headed for the bathroom. Just then, the door lock turned, and Frenchie came in carrying a tray with two sterling silver domes. He smiled widely and bowed politely as though he were the bellman, "Mademoiselle, dinner is served."

Monica actually felt relief to see him and chirped, "Merci, Monsieur". Her cordial French response surprised Jean-Marc as it did herself! They both sensed the levity but suppressed laughter. He set the tray on her bed and lifted the domes slightly off several plates while announcing, "Roasted duck, shrimp scampi, wild rice pilaf, steamed broccoli, a Mediterranean salad tossed with raspberry vinaigrette, sun-dried tomato bread, and a Saratoni Chardonnay for Mademoiselle." Suddenly,

Monica began salivating. Wanting him to leave her alone, she told Jean-Marc she was tired and would try to eat something later. He respected her request and left.

She went for the wine first. She poured herself a glass out of the chilled bottle. Quietly, as though she was sneaking, she removed the domes off all the plates and began to sample all that he had brought. She was famished. She ate nearly everything on the tray and drank nearly all the wine.

5 Work Hard-Play Less ✎

The palm trees outside their townhouse were strung with white mini lights just like all the others along the road that faced the ocean. Ricki had moved in with her dad when she accepted the research job with the National Oceanic Atmospheric Administration in September 2011. Living with Don felt odd at first like she was going backward in life. She had to keep reminding herself that she lived 12 years on her own, nearly two of those years with a man she had naively thought to marry. She now had her Ph.D., had finished one postdoc appointment and just landed the job she always wanted. Her father had wanted her to join the Navy, but her interests were more aligned to oceanography. He was disappointed that she wouldn't follow his footsteps in the military but was pleased with his daughter's sea-centered choice and supported her in all ways. Her high school counselor, Mrs. Teal, had suggested that she attend the Oregon

Institute of Marine Biology to pursue a career with NOAA which offered financial assistance through scholarships and grant programs. Her undergraduate courses were offered at the Oregon State University in Eugene, close enough to visit home on weekends. Sarah lived in Sage for the first year out of high school and wrote articles for the *Sage Brush Gazette* but then moved to Eugene to pursue a degree in journalism at the University of Oregon. They commuted home together on weekends until Ricki's upper division courses required her to be stationed at the Marine Biology Lab in Charleston, OR. In her sophomore year, she applied for and was a recipient of the NOAA Hollings Undergraduate Scholarship which supplied a generous stipend and a paid summer intern position at a NOAA facility in Juneau where she assisted in molecular analyses of bioluminescence in the fish Stoplight Loosejaw. She applied for another internship for the summer following graduation and was granted one, stationed with the MEGA Team at Southwestern Fisheries Science Center in Santa Cruz, CA. That's where she met Steve. After that everything became convoluted. She had dated a few guys at Oregon State but never had felt compelled by them to go deeper into relationship. Steve and she worked under the same Principle Investigator on the genetic pathway of luceriferase, the enzyme responsible for bioluminescence in *Metridia longa*, a marine copepod. Luciferase also gave it's illuminating property to fireflies and sea pansies, and strategies to genetically engineer this property in other organisms were already underway. Steve managed the MEGA lab and was responsible for ordering supplies and keeping the apparatus performing properly. He held a postdoc position studying various biological traits expressed by marine life, but his funding ran out in a year and a half and he would have to move on. They both knew that their career paths would probably separate them, but they got deeper involved anyway. She didn't suspect that she would fall in love, but she did. At the end of summer, she didn't want to move away from Steve. Her stipend had run out and her father wasn't willing to pay for her to stay in California just because she now had a boyfriend. He was afraid she was being derailed and was not supportive of her career status, lack of vision or ambition. She looked for lab work in Santa Cruz but found nothing. She was only an undergrad and most positions were granted to grad students. She finally found something at a popular aquarium in Monterey working as a docent. It wasn't research but helped pay rent and was only a 30-minute commute from Steve's small studio in Capitola.

At Christmas, instead of going home to Sage to see her dad, she flew to Spokane to meet Steve's parents. During the short time they were there, she felt landlocked and couldn't wait to get back to the ocean. She became very good at convincing herself that her life was on track and that she was happy. After the holidays, the routineness of life settled in and, to her surprise, she began to enjoy teaching the public about the immensity of the ocean and the value of marine life. On her lunch break, she frequently wandered over to the Hopkins Marine Laboratory to chat with people who spoke her language of biochemistry and genetics. The lab was a satellite of UC Stanford, much like Bodega Bay Marine Lab was of UC Davis and Scripps Institution of Oceanography was of UC San Diego. She became good friends with Sally who was a grad student studying contractile proteins in marine organisms at varied temperatures. Sally's research was in collaboration with the Kawelo Marine Laboratory in Hawaii which was part of the UH Pacific Biomedical Research Center. There was also a loose collaboration with the Max Planck Institute for Cell Biology in Germany as well. It was apparent that a great deal of Sally's funding originated from interest in medical advances and pharmaceutical companies.

Over the next year, Ricki became more interested in being in Monterey than in going home and spending time with Steve. Steve was generally not interested in talking about biology when he got home and only wanted to eat the dinner that she prepared every night and then fall asleep watching TV. It used to be that she never minded that he got loaded when he got home but now it bothered her. It was like an "off" switch that left him vacant – a body with no one inside. She was lonely and felt stranded like she had run aground. Her sense of malaise intensified as time passed. Steve sensed her unhappiness and, without much hesitation, intensified his search for a permanent position. The months dragged on but in November, he had two interviews: 1) another postdoctoral appointment at the Great Lakes Environmental Research Laboratory in Michigan where he would continue to work in genetics, and 2) a permanent position at NOAA's Pasco Research Station not far from Spokane where he would manage salmon passage up the Columbia River. He settled for the permanent position and moved to Kennewick, WA where he could be closer to his family. And that was the end of their relationship.

Ricki looked out the window at the palm trees along El Paso Grande anointed with specks of lights. Daylight was approaching. The street lights and the white mini-lights that were spiraled around the trees would shut off and the bustle of the day would begin. As people and cars began populating the street below, her mind mused about diurnal animals and the *'changing of the guard'* as she called it – when nocturnals went into their dark places and diurnals emerged, and how the phenomenon is regulated by genes interacting with earthly cues. The coffee was having the desired effect of jump-starting her brain as it segued from biorhythms and response to light into the topic of bioluminescence and other physical capabilities that marine organisms possessed. Sally had opened a whole world of possibilities for her, reigniting an obsessive interest in oceanic research. Sally was now an associate professor in the Pharmaceutical Science Department at the University of Hawaii, Hilo. She had several grad students in her lab continuing her research in contractile proteins and the potential use in medicine. They emailed each other occasionally but time and distance had managed to dilute their friendship as it faithfully seems to do. Sarah and she hadn't spoken in months. And Steve? Steve was altogether gone even though they agreed to keep in contact. She caught herself slipping into the '*I suck at relationships quagmire*' and promptly jumped out by shifting her thoughts to antifreeze proteins and strategies to continue investigating them. Her cell phone rang. She jumped to grab it and spilled coffee on her PJ bottoms, "Crap!" she cursed. "Oh, hi Dad. No, no, I wasn't sleeping. I just slopped Joe on myself reaching for the phone. I saw the weather and it said the D.C. area was getting hammered with an ice storm. When do you think you'll be coming home? It's still winter here, but nothing like there!" Her dad wasn't demonstrative in person but made up for it on the telephone. She hated it when he called her *'Darling'*, but she ignored it, "I miss you too, Dad."

The Flora and Fauna Genome Conference had been held every January in San Diego for 20 years. The initial conference was held in October and did not include animal research, but the organizers changed it to January so that Easterners could escape the mid-winter bitter cold. A few years later, animal genomics was added and the size of the meeting more than doubled. She had attended only a few times before, twice when she was in grad school at UC San Diego and one other time back when she was a postdoc at Oakridge in the ORNL Center for Molecular Physics. Those were miserable years for her so far from the ocean, but the postdoctoral appointment had served its purpose in helping her land her current position at NOAA. Lydia Tankersley had a large hand in it as well. Lydia was her mentor in antifreeze proteins at UCSD where Ricki had defended her thesis on AFPs in terrestrials. Lydia recently contacted Ricki to see if she would be interested in presenting a Keynote Lecture in her place at FFG XX, claiming she couldn't make the conference due to family obligations. Instead, a postdoc named Morgan would be presenting a poster on the biochemical effects of AFPs in mice ovaries. Ricki had met with Lydia and Morgan in early December where it was decided the Keynote lecture would be entitled *Subarctic*

Spruce Budworm AFPs Show High Thermal Hysteresis Activity. Ricki was hoping for high interest from Alaskan and Canadian pathologists.

6 Time Out ⋙

The lab phone rang and one of the grad students answered it. After a brief conversation, she held the phone up and loudly said, "It's for you, Dr. Tankersley".

"Hello, this is Dr. Tankersley."

"'Hi Lydia, it's me, Morgan. I wanted to check in before today's over. I will send you my final poster in a few minutes and if you have any edits, could you get them to me by 3:00? I need to pack and all that fun stuff."

"Yes, I'll get it right back to you. Remember, you are going there to accomplish three things: 1) to present the work we have accomplished, 2) learn as much as you can pertaining to our research and 3) make connections to forward your career. I'm meeting up with some friends from Memorial tomorrow night for dinner. You are welcome to join." Morgan thanked her but declined the invitation to which she replied, "Okay then. I'll see you in a few days."

"Oh, did you forget? Morgan interjected. "I'm going to Cabo after the meeting."

"Oops, yeah, I did forget. Well, have fun and be sure to drop the poster off at the lab before you go, okay?"

"Sure thing. And I'll see you in a couple weeks."

"See ya. Have fun in Cabo," and Lydia hung up.

She picked Shara up at school at 3:45. She was 15 minutes late and Shara was pissed off about it. Whenever Shara was angry at Lydia, her upper lip stuck out just like her father's. It was hard for Lydia to look at her daughter when she did this.

"So, how was school today, honey?"

"You should know," she seethed back, insolently.

"How should I know, Shara, you have to tell me. I know I am talented, but I've never been able to master the reading of minds."

The tension eased just a little bit as a smile crept up the sides of Shara's mouth. "All the kids are saying my mom went maniac on the principal."

"Oh, Shara, they're just jealous. They want their mommies to stand up for them in the principal's office. I swear Shara - if that kid touches you again, I will come to that school and rip his ears off. It's not smart to tick off a mama bear, Boo". Shara's smile could stretch from one ear to the other when her heart was in it. Her heart was in it.

It was the Saturday before the conference and Lydia drove Shara to Las Vegas to spend a long weekend with her dad. The school had scheduled a staff day for Monday which Lydia thought was ridiculous because the kids just returned from a two-week Christmas break. She booked a room at a resort at Lake Las Vegas where she planned to catch up on reading journal articles and getting a massage. Carl was cordial when they arrived at his house in West Sahara and offered an invitation to join him and Shara for lunch and a gondola ride at the Venetian, but she didn't want to encroach on their one-on-one time. Shara saw her father only about once a month because his weekends climbing at Red Rocks with his buddies was a high priority for him. He claimed that weekend recreation is how he kept his sanity after being in litigation all week and that when Shara got older, he could teach her to golf, ski and climb and they would have great fun together.

Lydia got back on the beltway which took her directly to East Lake Mead Parkway. She plopped on the bed and took a short nap. It was noon when she woke, ordered in-room for a bottle of sauvignon blanc and read several articles before her scheduled massage. A weekend of relaxation was past due and she thought of the book, *Eat,*

Pray, Love by Elizabeth Gilbert. Smiling, she renamed it, 'Read, Sleep, Publish'.

By Sunday, she was completely relaxed and hardly thought about Shara, the divorce, or rises in college tuition. She spent as much time as possible at poolside, baking in the Mojave sun and sipping Moscow Mules. She wished that she had more days of being a lizard instead of just one more and asked the front desk for a late Monday checkout.

On Monday morning, she ate breakfast in the hotel restaurant and as she passed the Concierge Desk, she was offered the *Las Vegas Tribune,* but she opted instead for the *San Diego Review* and the *San Francisco Inquisitor.* She scolded herself for not being more gracious to the Concierge while refusing his offer. Dr. Karrington had asked her to practice choosing her words more carefully, intentionally acknowledging people's kindness and to respond in a way that rewarded them for that kindness. He said that people, in some professional fields and because of social media, had lost basic social skills. Lydia understood Dr. Karrington's observation and committed to his suggestion, if for nothing else, for Shara's sake. She doubted her ability to completely modify how she interacted with a world that seemed to always be focused on trivial matters. Her mother, now dead almost 22 years, used to always quote, "You can't change the spots on a leopard." Sometimes she was referring to other people, sometimes she was referring to Lydia. She smiled, thinking about all the quips and quotes her mother used to whip out, most of which stung her delicate younghood.

After breakfast, she stopped by the hotel desk to arrange for one more night's stay. Carl had cancelled all his Tuesday appointments and Lydia had nothing pressing except dinner with her friends at Fio's, which she decided to forfeit. She had a slight concern for Shara's school attendance but that soon dissolved with the dismissive recognition that Shara did not belong to them. Lydia looked forward to one more day swimming, reading and storing UV rays like a solar battery.

7 The Imposter ❧

When Monica awoke, it was pitch black and she jerked up, grabbing at her throat. There were no strings there. No cuffs around her feet. She heard birds chirping in the courtyard below where sun lovers hovered near the pool like hummingbirds near a feeder. Beyond the courtyard, she could see only brown hills and scrub brush. The terrain could be Nevada, or southern CA, it was impossible to tell. The tray was still on the bed where she had left it the night before. The Bible was on the floor next to the bed, but she had no recollection how it got there. She felt groggy but well rested and relaxed. She wondered how long it would be before Jean-Marc turned the lock in the door and what would happen this day. She thought about whether to tell them again she wasn't Lomax. It seemed weird to her that they hadn't figured it out yet. They had removed her room key from her pocket and if they had respectable investigative skills, they would have sent someone to the hotel to locate her pack and I.D. They must be relying only on the two men who witnessed her putting up her poster. She tried to remember the events leading up to her abduction. *Abduction - listen to me. Is this really happening to me? Abducted. Me?* Somewhere inside she was unbelieving still. She ignored her inner prodding, afraid she would cave in to helplessness. She forced herself to think about the conference. She remembered registering, running into Dana and Pederik and going to put up her poster. *Someone was in her spot. It had annoyed her. She read the poster name and author. The author was Lomax. First name?* She recalled it was maybe a male name and the title something about antifreeze proteins in mice. *That's a strange combination,* she mused, *why would mice need antifreeze proteins?* She made herself think about that night again. She had decided to put her poster up in Lomax's spot instead of fussing over such a petty issue as a board number. Two men walked by and stopped at the end of the row of posters, conferring with one another. *One of them was...* "One of them was Jean-Marc!" she said out loud. "That's why they assume I am Lomax? How idiotic! They saw me put up my poster on ubiquitin, yet they just went by board numbers. I'm in this predicament because they are morons! My nametag is in the bag with my conference program. Where is that?"

It was now already Tuesday and the conference ended on Thursday. If she were to tell her captors that she is not

Lomax, what would they do? She could fake the thermal hysteresis thing for only a brief time – a very brief time. The most she knew about antifreeze proteins and the phenomena of thermal hysteresis was confined to earlier studies in a fish that could endure temperatures as low as -1.9^0 C in Arctic seas. She learned this as an undergraduate at Humboldt State University 12 years ago. She didn't follow that body of research and had no clue why the proteins were now found in mice or why anyone, including these jerks, would be interested in them. Monica decided to tell them that she was not the one they were interested in.

She took a shower, dried her hair with a towel and put her wrinkled clothes back on. There was a knock on the door and the sound of a key in the lock. Frenchie came in and without his usual charm said, "It's time to talk about your work, Ms. Lomax. I'll take this tray." He left as coldly as he came. Monica was shaking when the door opened again. Frenchie smiled warmly and held his hand out as though to thoughtfully escort his date. His returned charm calmed her nerves and she said, "You have the wrong person. I don't know anything about the process of thermal hysteresis!" Frenchie chuckled. Monica, desperate to be saved, started reciting prayers she learned in catechism a lifetime ago.

𝟴 Like Riding a Bicycle ⚘

There were empty bottles of wine and some dirty plates from room service on the table near the bed. Outside, there were big puff clouds hanging like fat sheep in the winter sky. Mike went downstairs to a brightly illuminated lobby that smelled of waffles and burnt toast, dispensed coffee into a disposable cup, checked out and drove south on I-580 until it coalesced with 395 in Carson City. He thought about going to Yosemite but as he arrived at the turnoff, he saw the sign reporting that Tuolumne Pass was still closed. Thus far, it had been a winter of few storms and despite the warm temperatures, the melt-off on the east side of the Sierras was slower than usual. The Owens River mildly meandered through the valley, and the banks were peppered here and there with fly fishermen bundled up, wading in the flow. Mike used to fish with his dad when he was a kid, and always thought he would get back to it one day. Instead he had fashioned a life in a metropolis, fishing for the big story. And there were aplenty that had gotten away. He grinned at the metaphor he just coined and made a mental note to remember it for future writings. He got a room in Bishop and found the local liquor store where he bought a California fishing license, a cheap flyrod kit, some tippet, a handful of flies and sunblock. The owner, Fred, tried to sell him some neoprene waders but Mike decided that he would be happy to fish from the bank. Instead he bought some wading boots and neoprene socks for walking through the muck and traversing small tributaries that meandered through the pastures.

Fishing came back easily to him. He was able to land a few browns on his first day using wooly buggers. Despite the fact it was early January, there was a short *Baetis* mayfly hatch early Saturday afternoon just as Fred had predicted. Blue Winged Olive emergers worked like magic, imitating molting mayflies stuck in the surface film. While casting from the eastern bank near Lone Pine, the sun sank low, sharply defining Mount Whitney against the western sky and for the first time since the bombing, Mike forgot about Gwynn.

The headlines for Tuesday's *Review* was devoted to a big story about the airport and Eastwest Airlines. On the bottom right of the front page, however, Lydia saw an article entitled, "Woman Suspected Missing at Mission Valley Conference." Her attention piqued as she read that Monica Linden, a Ph.D. research associate from the USDA-Agricultural Research Service in Albany, CA failed to meet with colleagues as scheduled Sunday night. The article went on to say that she had checked into the *Shine and Explore Hotel* Sunday afternoon and had plans for dinner with friends but never showed up. Her friends had repeatedly called her room to locate her. Her sister, Tanya Long, of San Leandro, California said Linden was not returning her calls which was highly unusual. Monday morning, Dr. Linden's conference registration materials were found on the conference center grounds in the rear parking lot. As Lydia read through the rest of the article, she heard a male ordering lunch at a table nearby. His voice was thick with a French accent as he ordered a California Club sandwich and an IPA. He asked the waiter to bring him the San Diego paper. A little bit later she heard him sigh, click his tongue and utter under his breath, "Too bad. Too bad."

She decided to risk taking the 15 toward Los Angeles since it was mid-day Tuesday and not peak traffic hours. If it were Sunday or Monday, she would've chosen an alternate route to avoid gnarled traffic. It would have taken longer, but her nerves would've been happier. Getting caught in gridlock only made her mad at Carl for moving so far away.

On Wednesday while dropping Shara off at school, Lydia's ringtone began chiming in her purse. Her daughter and she were engaged in smiles and kisses as Shara hopped out of the front seat, so she let the call go to voicemail. She was hoping that the long weekend with her father would help Shara forget about the previous week and the incident with Bobby Sanders. Shara ran into the crowd of kids as though she had no care in the world. Lydia smiled then pulled the Passat forward into a turnout to check her cell phone. It was Dr. Karrington's receptionist leaving a voicemail that her appointment this Wednesday would need to be rescheduled. Lydia had decided to work at home the next few days so she could work on the review paper that she had been pecking away at for the last 10 months. Morgan would be in Cabo for another two weeks and everyone else would be busy at FFG. She felt a sort of abandonment. She then realized it was self-imposed abandonment, and that she could make it work for her.

She never called Dr. Karrington back to reschedule, deciding she needed a break in self-improvement. Working at home the week of the conference had been greatly rewarding. For the first time in a long time, she had been on her own clock except for driving Shara to and from school. On Monday morning, she received a call from Ricki O'Connor. She figured Ricki most likely wanted to discuss AFPs and her keynote seminar. "Hi Ricki. How'd it go? The keynote?"

"It went great," Ricki answered. "There were a couple questions from the audience which told me that, at least some people knew what thermal hysteresis was! As far as the concurrent sessions, I jumped around a lot, trying to catch talks that were pertinent to our research. I find myself more and more getting tugged away from ocean organisms because we keep discovering the same genes and proteins act similarly in terrestrial organisms. It's a game changer and I'm not liking it much."

Lydia responded in mentor fashion, "Orthologous verses homologous. It's good to keep your mind open, Ricki. I'm glad I don't care what direction my research takes me – land, ocean, Argentina."

"Argentina? What are you talking about?" Ricki said.

"Oh, I'm just being funny. I really don't care much about where I live. Now, you? You freak out if you're not near an ocean."

"It's true. It's so true. It's definitely my Achille's heel," Ricki said and then added, "Did you hear about the researcher from ARS that went missing?"

"Yeah. I saw it in the paper."

"Have you talked to Morgan? Did he post his presentation in the wrong spot?"

"Morgan is in Cabo with some friends and not due back for a couple weeks."

There was a lapse in conversation and then Ricki said, "The newspaper said that Morgan may have been the actual target and that Linden was kidnapped by mistake."

"What? Do you know how absurd that sounds?"

"Yeah, I do. I really do. It's like some buffoon crime boss," Ricki mocked, "'oops! wrong victim'".

Lydia laughed while silently surfing through the talk titles in each concurrent session of the online program. As she expected, the bulk of the research presented at the conference was redundant with last year's presentations. *Same people, same news, same views. How far can a person further their research in just one year?* Lydia had suggested to the organizers that it would be advantageous to hold the conference every other year, but they disagreed because by not having the meeting annually, the venue would nearly double the charge on everything from poster board rentals to continental breakfasts to ice water pitchers. It was like venue-promotional blackmail. So, Lydia had decided she would skip every other year. When Ricki finally stopped talking, Lydia ended the call, claiming she had a department meeting soon.

What Ricki had said about Monica Linden rankled her. She looked up the poster numbers on the conference web site and discovered that Monica Linden's poster on ubiquitin in tomato was indeed next to Morgan's poster on antifreeze proteins in mice. She sent a text to Morgan but did not receive a reply. She was concerned that he may be in danger but didn't want to raise a red flag just yet. She remembered he wouldn't be back in the lab for another week. She sent another text message asking him to reply ASAP. She also asked one of her grad students to send him a message on social media in case he was posting photos to friends and family. She went to the lab for the rest of the morning until attending a department meeting at 1:00. Her cell buzzed while in the meeting and she saw it was a text from Morgan, "Hey Lydia, what's up? Did you find our poster on my desk?" She texted back, hiding her phone under the table, "Just making sure u made it to ur fun destination. Pls call me when u r back. Want to hear about ur successes at FFG. - L". She was relieved he was fine and scolded herself for being such a mother hen. It was precisely that nature that caused her to not mention the news about the Linden kidnapping. Whatever the reason for the kidnapping, she felt he was safe in Mexico. Two hours later, her phone alarm went off, notifying her it was almost time to pick up Shara. They stopped at the bowling alley on the way home to play a game and have French fries and cola. Shara had a good day at school and Lydia was looking forward to a fun night at home. *Oh, God, how she loved being with her!* It was 6:30 when they arrived home and she didn't notice the dark grey SUV parked a few houses down.

10 From Pot to Frying Pan ✍

He stayed in Bishop two weeks, each day more cherished than the one before. His newfound joy and peace were interrupted frequently with pangs of guilt for forsaking the anguish that had enveloped him just two weeks prior. The temperatures remained mild, the hatches became predictable and the banks of the river became increasingly crowded with territorial anglers very serious about their sport. The calm waters of the Owens River no longer felt like a haven. As he drove south out of town, he thought how his choice to linger and fish had been a very good decision and he vowed to continue the sport even after he went back to San Francisco. It had made him feel whole, like he had gone home somewhere inside. To a timeless place where days were lazy and insects predictably swarmed in the warm rays of the afternoon sun.

The drive to Palm Springs wasn't filled with anguish like on the previous leg of his trip. He figured that if he could discover an island of joy like flyfishing, then there must be other discoveries waiting for him. He cringed at the underthought that he was thinking like an *experience-junkie* - the kind of person who is so shallow, so narcissistic that they make no commitments, no long-term plans and have no lasting relationships. They live life only for the thrill of the moment and die lonely. He had met many people like that in his line of work. He pushed the negative thought out, as he reminded himself that *he had a job and a career and had just lost the biggest commitment of his life.* It was winter in the Sonoran Desert and the vegetation was barely showing the buds that would soon burst back into life.

His phone started vibrating in his pocket as he was getting a bite to eat at a burger joint in Ridgecrest. It was Fogerty, his boss. He didn't answer the call, figuring a text message would follow. He rationalized, *he was on vacation – a vacation that Fogerty had insisted he take – and now Fogerty was yanking his chain.* He finished his burger and tapped the contact link for the Adonnia Hotel in Palm Springs. The Spanish style of this lodge intrigued him, and he hoped he could visit the driving range of the nearby country club. He also wanted to ride the tram and hike in the Joshua Tree National Park. Carolyn had said both were spectacular in the winter or spring before it got hot. His phone vibrated again, and it was Fogerty leaving a text message: "Mike, I know I encouraged you to take some time off, but you are going to want to hear this. Call me."

Mike pulled off I-40 and into a gas station in Barstow. Just when he turned off the car, he got another text, this one from Sarah that said "Urgent. Call Fogerty." He knew if Sarah wanted him to call, it must be important. He autodialed his boss and got his voicemail. "Hi Jeff, Mike returning your call. I'm getting gas in Barstow. Will be on the road soon. Call me back." He then called Sarah.

She picked up. "How are you doing, Mike?

"There are good times, then there are bad times," he answered. Then citing the Charles Dicken's quote in a dramatic voice, he added, "It was the best of times, it was the worst of times." He knew Sarah would laugh. She did. It was reporter code language for being under pressure in a world of deadlines, and sometimes, dead-end stories.

Sarah replied, "Mike, I got a lead on the SFO bombing. It's not much and it's an isthmus conjecture but I thought you might want in on it."

"What you got?"

"A woman's body was discovered at a construction site on Hwy 93 west of Hoover Dam. Dental records have confirmed a Monica Linden, a genetic research associate of

ARS in Albany, CA."

"Refresh me, what is ARS?"

"It stands for Agricultural Research Service. USDA. She researched tomato genomics."

"So, why would this have any dire interest to me right now?"

"The FBI thinks her abduction is tied to Neptune."

Gwynn's face flashed in front of him, heat consumed him, and his vision contracted. He asked Sarah to tell Fogerty to expect a callback when he got to his hotel in Palm Springs.

"Okay, Mike. I will. But I am flying to Las Vegas in the morning to investigate. If you don't feel you are up to it, just let me go ahead. But, if that is how you choose, I will be the lead on the story. Call me tonight after you talk with Fogerty."

Mike was stunned. He pulled away from the gas pumps and parked near the bathrooms. He sat, wondering what he should do. He felt he was just beginning to see his way back to life, and now he is being called to look back into death. Into disaster. Into violence, hatred and ugliness. He wasn't sure he was ready. And even more disturbing, he wasn't sure he was cut out for the job anymore.

As he opened his suitcase in his hotel room, Mike wondered if, indeed, his post-traumatic stress would make him one of those guys - an *experience junkie*. He now could see how it happens. Half of him wanted to remain in recreation mode and half of him wanted to go back to work, but only to find the bastards that killed Gwynn. Very little of him wanted '*the story*'. He slipped on his swim trunks and found the jacuzzi. He needed the experience of warm soothing water. A familiar womb. Thankfully, there were no Marco Polo children.

He returned to his room and donned some sweatpants and a hoodie. He picked up his phone and called Fogerty. He hadn't come any further in resolving how to respond to the opportunity presented to him. He had learned to call everything an '*opportunity*', a lesson he learned in Sunday School growing up in the Ozarks. A challenge could be viewed as something negative - a threat, a chore, too hard, boring. Or it could be viewed as an '*opportunity*' - a test of your capabilities. As a young teenager, that perspective had got him in trouble when some peers challenged him to jump 20 feet down into the quarry pond. That opportunity landed him in a hospital for a week of treatment for chemical exposure. Some opportunities are traps and it is difficult sometimes to know when that is the case. That is what Mike found himself pondering as he waited for Fogerty to pick up.

"Hey, Mike. Glad to hear your voice. You are doing okay?" Before Mike had a chance to answer, Fogerty continued, "Something came across my desk and Sarah is already jumping on it. It has to do with Neptune and I thought you would want the opportunity to work on it if you wanted to."

There was that tricky word *'opportunity'*.

Fogerty continued, "A woman attending the Flora and Fauna Genome Conference in San Diego was kidnapped and killed for what the FBI believes is related to research on thermal hysteresis."

Mike interrupted, "Say what?"

Fogerty went on, "Thermal hysteresis. It's the process by which proteins in certain animals suppress the freezing of their tissue in sub-freezing conditions. Fish in Alaska, for instance. Antifreeze proteins, a.k.a. AFPs, inhibit ice crystal formation within cells. Anyway, the FBI became involved because it was a kidnapping and when they discovered that the poster presentations were switched at the conference, they…."

"Hold on. What'd'ya mean the posters were switched?" Mike interrupted again.

"A postdoc from UC San Diego put his poster on a Monica Linden's assigned board. The FBI think that the perps thought Linden was doing research on antifreeze proteins in mice when actually she was reporting research on something relating to tomatoes."

"In mice? Research for human application?"

"Yes. That is the thought right now. I have a phone number for a Mr. McElroy at the FBI who thinks that this is connected to Neptune and the SFO bombing."

"Mike, are you still there?"

"Yes," Mike said quietly. "I have McElroy's phone number in my wallet. He interviewed me at the hospital. Jeff, I've been trying to regain my footing and I'm not sure I am ready to go back into investigations. The opportunity to nail those who killed Gwynn is a tempting one, I'm just not sure it's a good idea. I could end up in jail if my revenge takes on a life of its own. I'm in uncharted territory and not sure what's next."

"Those are wise words, Mike. I just thought I would be remiss if I didn't offer you the opportunity. Sarah will call you tomorrow after she gets settled in Las Vegas. Since you already have established rapport with McElroy, you should take the lead. Uh, that is if you decide to get in. Good-night Mike."

"Good-night Jeff. And Jeff, thank you. For everything."

He thought about Sarah's comment about taking the story lead. *She should have it. That would take the pressure off me and I could focus on the case for the right reasons. There are dangerous people running loose in the name of the environment and they need to be stopped.* He reflected on the field of journalism, *News media and reporters play an important role in the fabric of our society and have a responsibility. Many have died seeking The Truth. It's like a Holy Grail. Only, once you find it, you sell it… and then follow up by initiating a search for yet another chalice. The cycle is endless, and some reporters burn out, tiring of the game. These Truths are swallowed up daily by the public only to fade into obscurity like an ignited match that is brilliant for a moment and then tossed away, flame exhausted.* Exhausted. He was exhausted. Damaged, lonely and exhausted.

11 Serendipity

Ricki was glad the FFG conference was over and the keynote lecture behind her. Her morning conversation with Lydia had made her want to focus on marine research and not on tree of life debates or public appearances. She didn't give a rip about either of those. Her lab in La Jolla was delving into characterization of several types of antifreeze proteins from both polar oceans. It appeared that, despite their similarity in structure, the proteins that protected cells from ice crystal formation evolved independent of each other. Convergent evolution was a topic that many geneticists downplayed in favor of divergent evolution. Homology in housekeeping genes across myriad taxa exhilarated primordial soup proponents, who liked to construct phylogenetic bootstrapped dendrograms to describe the tree of life. However, in this case, similar antifreeze proteins evolved under the same selection pressure in different geographic locations to express similar resistance mechanisms to freezing temperatures. Dissimilar paths to an identical outcome. To some extent, this paradigm supports Creationists' claim that organisms did not originate from a single lineage. Ricki didn't care about who begat who or when. She was amazed about the complex labyrinth of life and studying it was a form of worship for her. She wasn't sure where it all began. She figured she wasn't there in the beginning and she will never know the truth for certain until she dies. Furthermore, she saw no benefit in knowing how it all began. Her interest in antifreeze proteins was not unlike Sally's interest in contractile proteins. She knew AFPs had an important role to play in our society and she felt it was her duty to discover whatever that was and advance the benefit. That was NOAA's service mandate.

She rode her bike to the laboratory where she discussed lab supply orders with Marjorie, the lab manager. A thermocycler was not ramping properly, causing spurious annealing to the target template and she gave authorization to order a new one. A grad student whose thesis was on mollusk hybrid swarm populations that were forming, hypothetically, because of oceanic temperature fluctuations, cornered Ricki at the coffee pot to ask if she could purchase some Long-PCR *Taq* polymerase to amplify across three adjacent mitochondrial loci. Standing in front of the shelf unit that held an array of thermocyclers, Ricki marveled out loud to Marjorie yet another time about the remarkable combination of a serendipitous discovery of a bacterium living in a Yellowstone National Park hot spring and an LSD-induced revelation by a postdoc on a road trip and how it catapulted molecular biology into the next generation. PCR (polymerase chain reaction) revolutionized biotechnology by reproducing exact replicas of a template DNA using single nucleotides and the precious Yellowstone-derived thermostable enzyme in a three-step thermal process. Marjorie politely listened, nodded in affirmation and then informed Ricki that maintenance on the autoclave and the still were both due and the upright -80° C freezer was full to capacity, which meant it was time to either purge archived material or buy an additional freezer. Ricki said that she would need to look at her equipment budget for the year and it was possible that the freezer expense could be picked up by Facilities.

After an hour she was able to settle down at her own bench in the lab. She really didn't have too much going on, but she loved being in the lab and spent time there reading articles. She felt it was important for her lab to see her in the trenches with them. It kept communication lines open and they respected her for that. She ate a bag lunch on the patio with the others and, afterwards, went to her office where she had a quarterly budget projection to prepare and return five phone calls.

She checked her cell phone for messages and discovered that her dad had called while she was outside eating lunch and left a message saying he would be home tomorrow. It was Tuesday and she hadn't heard from him in two weeks. His voice sounded distant, removed. She tried calling him back and left a voice message, "Hi Dad. I'm so glad you are coming home."

12 Addicted to the Hunt ◆

The next morning, he grabbed the paper from the concierge and drove to the Palm Springs Tram. The air was crisp but held the promise of a warm afternoon. The vista was incredible and lifted his spirits as he remembered the time his father had taken him and his brother up to the top of a fire lookout near Thornfield, Missouri. His brother had commented that he loved the Ozarks and would never leave them. And he hadn't. He settled in a little town called Ava. Mike had gone to visit him and his family five years before Georgia was killed in a car accident. She had been driving home from choir practice when she fell asleep. The kids were almost grown and Derek had to finish raising them on his own. Mike suggested they relocate in California and get a fresh start, but he said he wasn't ready to leave the mountains and all their friends. Mike never asked again. Derek seemed happy where he was. In some ways, Mike envied him. Maybe he would take a trip home when this thing is all over. He caught himself, what did he mean 'all over'? I guess that meant he was going to embrace the *opportunity.* The view and the food were divine as Carolyn had said and he consumed it with intention as though it was his last supper. He finished his glass of cabernet franc as the waiter took his plate away. On the way down the tram, his cell phone rang. It was Sarah. Without hesitation he blurted it out, "I'll do it. I'm in." As he said it, he remembered the moment he jumped into the toxic quarry pool.

He didn't have time to go hiking in Joshua Tree National Park as he had hoped but decided to drive through it even though it added some miles to his trip to Henderson. Pinto Basin Road was mostly deserted once he got past Cottonwood visitor center. He had picked up a sandwich, beer and more water at a mini mart before leaving Palm Springs. Warm beer wasn't his favorite, but he relished the idea of sitting in the middle of nowhere, sipping on a bottle of beer before he dove back into the *'jaws of the tiger'*. This was a phrase he and his cohorts at the newspaper had adopted for being strung out on a relentless hunt. It was an addiction, no less than that of the *experience junkie*. He was amused over this revelation of hypocrisy while sipping on a warm IPA at Arch Rock. He, too, was a junkie. When he reached Hwy 95 it was already 2:00. He figured he'd get to the hotel where Sarah was staying by 6:00. He sent her a text to say he'd meet her for dinner.

He couldn't tell if Sarah looked frazzled or energized as she walked towards his table. He had ordered a bottle of wine and was already feeling the wanted effect. He had asked the host of the hotel restaurant for a large table knowing he would be writing on his tablet. A lot of younger reporters had adopted the habit of writing notes in their phones, but he was old school. He believed old gum shoe detective ways always paid off. He knew a colleague who had lost a whole day's worth of interviews recorded on his phone before he had time to synchronize it with his laptop. Ironically, that was the same reporter who poked fun at Mike for using tablets, calling him "Columbo". Sarah grabbed Mike's right hand, squeezed it and asked how he was doing. Her warmth cut, and he felt tears come into his eyes.

"I'm not sure, Sarah. I think I am doing fine and then - whammo! anger, rage, helplessness, sorrow, defeat – all these emotions well up like a tsunami that slams me against a rock in a broken heap. It's really weird. I thought I was fine until I saw you walk in."

She didn't say anything just kept holding his hand looking at his face, reading it. He felt a peculiar sense of peace flow over him, his heart calmed by something in her grey eyes. His wild emotions were calmed by her presence. He had worked with Sarah for several years but had never noticed this quality in her before. She had some sort of power, a gift. She let go of his hand, sat down and poured herself a glass of wine.

Smiling she asked, "So, what have you been doing, Mike? It sounds like you have been seeing some sights."

Mike told her about flyfishing on the Owens River in an unseasonably warm winter with unseasonal hatches. He talked about how it brought back memories of his Ozark home and dad. Sarah shared that she lure-fished lakes with childhood friends when she was growing up in Oregon. Dinner came, and they continued the small talk until their plates were cleared by the waitress and the notebooks came out. Sarah opened her spiral notepad and began to fill Mike in on the story.

"The FBI think that there was a man on board the airplane that was the target of the explosion. It wasn't a random bombing or a statement bombing. At first they thought it was the work of an eco-terrorist group called Neptune."

Mike interrupted, "Yes, Agent McElroy told me that they claimed responsibility for the bombing. I looked online at their website and asked if you could do some research on them. That was before I left town."

"Well, Neptune was reported to claim responsibility, but it came out that they only supported resistance to the man that was targeted. They didn't target the plane." Sarah said.

"So, *BFE News* didn't get the story right? What was their source?" Mike interrupted.

"Shh, Shh. Let me finish." Sarah reciprocated. "A call came in to the FBI, from someone claiming that Neptune was claiming responsibility. A trace on the call showed that the call was made from Manitoba. Neptune is an international organization with offices in Canada but not in Manitoba. Only coastal provinces. Before the trace, *BFE* jumped on the report, trying to beat its competitors. You know how it is these days, everyone leaping before they look just to get an edge. Fogerty called Agent McElroy to report to him what I had discovered about Neptune - you remember? You asked me to research their website. The FBI was way ahead of me, but I discovered that Neptune has become a bonified NGO. They no longer advocate or support radical activity. They hire scientists and have an outreach program that offers grants and educational opportunities to young adults. That doesn't mean to say that some of their members didn't jump ship and start an offshoot of the old eco group. The FBI have member names before-and-after the split and are watching cell and social media communications. McElroy told us that it appears that the target in the bombing was a corporate executive of an oil company based in Houston called Rangor, Inc. Rangor has been providing funding to and collaborating with Oak Ridge National Laboratory in Advanced Materials research at the Center for Molecular Biophysics at the University of Tennessee. Their research spans anything from the reuse of rubber tires to medical uses for scorpion venom. The question is, what is Rangor really interested in developing and why?" Sarah took a breath, deciding where to go next with her narrative. Mike waited patiently even though his interrogative nature was dying to take control and ask a plethora of questions.

Sarah continued, "The forensic lab in Quantico, Virginia is still processing evidence from the airport, but a briefcase was recovered from the wreckage that they believe was Mr. Auckman's." Sarah could see Mike was about to interrupt, so quickly added, "Mr. Auckman was a Rangor executive and the believed target on the plane." Sarah was making an effort to not use Gwynn's name when speaking of the plane bombing, knowing it would derail Mike's reporter instincts and his ability to follow her narrative. "There were fragments of documents recovered from the briefcase and Trace in Quantico is attempting to piece together some clues."

Mike couldn't suppress his questions any longer. He was now a goner, hook, line and sinker, "Did they ask Rangor or Oak Ridge what they were working on?"

Sarah sized up Mike, knowing that she probably was not going to be the first author on the story. She could see he was already taking the lead. She knew her mentor well enough to know that he was already in the jaws.

They ordered dessert and coffee and continued talking until the restaurant closed. Sarah explained how while the FBI was inching along on these leads, Monica Linden was kidnapped from a molecular biology conference and her body found at a construction site not far from Hoover Dam. She let Mike ask the questions and she answered them until he was caught up on everything she knew to date. He made diagrams on his notepad and took copious notes. He didn't fall asleep until two in the morning, searching for possible connections between Rangor, Inc., Advanced Materials, Monica Linden, ubiquitin in tomato, antifreeze proteins in mice, poster board switching, eco-terrorists, oil company, Canada. The kaleidoscope of mental fragments rolled him into a vortex of vexed slumber.

Morning came unwelcomed, sunlight shining through the drapes and his cell phone buzzing with the arrival of a text message. It was Sarah saying she was going down to grab some breakfast. He groaned. He replied he'd be down after he showered and shaved.

Her dark blond hair was pulled back in a ponytail which poked out through a hole in the back of her Giants cap. Sarah was plain compared to many women who lived in the city. Her simple charm and unpretentious manner were refreshing, and he looked forward to spending the day with her. He grabbed some grapefruit juice, a bagel and some black coffee from the continental breakfast counter and sat down across from her. She was studying an article in the *Las Vegas Tribune*

"Sarah, what's up?" Mike said as he gulped his juice. He liked to drink coffee after grapefruit juice because somehow it could make even the worst tasting coffee taste good.

"An article on Linden's kidnapping and murder."

"How much information is in it?"

"Not much. Less than what we know."

"I'm not completely up to speed on all the evidence yet and I still have questions."

"Nobody is. The body was found only a few days ago in the foundation of a wildlife overcrossing being constructed over Hwy 93 just east of here."

Mike was perplexed about the need for an overcrossing for animals. "I'm not following."

"You know, the things mob movies are made of… dumping Johnny, the Boss's nephew, in the abutment foundation of a bridge, then pouring cement over it."

"No, no. I get that. I mean why a bridge for animals?"

"Evidently, bighorn sheep are a big deal in this part of the country. Their migratory paths are interrupted by highways and interstates that prohibit their movement to find water, resources and to mate and disperse."

Sarah saw the look of dismay on Mike's face. Before he could speak, she continued, "Have you seen a vehicle that has struck a big horn sheep, Mike? Let me just put it this way, animals and vehicles do not belong on the same path. Da humans dey go dis-a-way and da animals dey go dat-a-way and no one gets hurt." She was grinning at him.

Mike objected, "Yeah, but our taxpayer dollars are going to towards this sort of thing rather than fighting crime, or feeding the poor, or even resurfacing our existing highways? It's a little bizarre if you ask me."

"Well, I'm glad nobody's asking you then." She laughed and winked at him, making him feel like a dinosaur. He wasn't that much older than she was, only six years or so. Yet, it was enough to display some disparity in core values – values that could partly be attributed to where one grew up, either a red state or a blue state. He was from a red state and it showed sometimes, despite his living in San Francisco for nearly ten years. Sarah continued, "The Federal Highway Administration reports that wildlife-vehicle collisions cost the United States 8.3 billion dollars per year. That includes everything: medical, funeral, burial, disability, auto repair, insurance company premium increases, road repair, carcass removal and disposal, the list goes on with a domino effect. The Western Governors Association signed an MOU with the DOI, DOE, and DOA in 2009 vowing to mitigate barriers to wildlife movement and reduce the number of wildlife-vehicle collisions."

Mike looked perplexed, "How do you know all this?"

"I did a piece on it last year. I'm hurt you didn't notice. I spent four months researching."

Mike smirked, knowing she was feigning hurt feelings, and waved his hand, "How old was this Linden woman, and was she fully clothed when found?"

"LVMPD claimed she wasn't raped. She was 32. Lived in Albany less than a mile from where she worked at ARS, USDA-Agriculture Research Service."

"LVMPD? Isn't this a federal case?"

"NDOT construction personnel didn't know it was the missing Monica Linden. They called 911. LVMPD responded. The LVMPD Crime Lab is one of the best in the west. Her DNA came up in CODIS as a Missing Persons case and then the game changed. When McElroy found out that there was a mix up in posters at the FFG...."

"What's FFG again?"

"Flora and Fauna Genome – the conference. When McElroy found out that the poster next to Monica's was one on antifreeze proteins, he became suspicious that there could be a case of mistaken identity and that this could be related to Rangor's interest in biophysics. It's all still up in the air right now."

"So, what's next for us?" Mike said, taking his final slug of coffee.

"We hunt."

Hoover Dam looked just the same as it did when he was a kid. His parents had taken him and his brother on vacation to *Dreamland* in California and they had seen several landmarks on the way. Hoover Dam was one of them. He remembered as a child being scared on top of the dam, looking down at the power plant below. Now, there was a bridge that circumvented the dam. They took a quick drive over the dam, turned around and drove back to the discovery site where the wildlife overcrossing was being built. Mike pulled his car off the road into a staging area for construction. Several of Nevada's Department of Transportation trucks were parked in the turnout and men with orange vests and white hardhats were standing around a dormant backhoe, drinking their morning coffee. The NDOT employees stopped kicking the dirt when Mike and Sarah approached them. One of them hollered, "Hey, no one is allowed here. It's off limits to the public." As the men dispersed, Mike noticed a LVMPD unit parked behind the truck and yellow crime scene tape stretching across a large area to the south. Mike and Sarah made their way back to the car where they sat silent for a few moments. Mike broke the silence first, "Tell me again, how did Monica die?"

"Bullet. To the back of the head." Sarah answered. Before Mike could ask the next question, she added, "Not here. She didn't die here."

"Primary?"

"Undiscovered to my knowledge."

"Close range?"

"Yes."

"Hopefully, she never saw it coming," Mike said ruefully. He thought how Gwynn had no idea her life would end in a flash.

When they got back to the hotel, they went to their rooms to catch up on emails, voicemails and texts. These days you were never off the clock thanks to technology. Smart phones were a boon to investigative reporters. You never needed to find a computer to search the web. Maps, databases, email and all sorts of useful apps were just a click away. Sarah went to her room to call Fogerty and to surf ARS's department webpages. Mike pulled out a dog-eared business card with an FBI emblem and left a voicemail with Agent McElroy asking him to call him back. He didn't need to wait long.

"Yeah, Agent McElroy, thank you for calling me back. I am in Las Vegas researching the Monica Linden case with Sarah, a co-worker from the *Inquisitor*. I was wondering if 1) you have any news on the airport bombing that killed my fiancée, and 2) how much can you tell me about the kidnapping and murder of Ms. Linden? Jeff Fogerty mentioned that you think there might be a connection between the two incidents. That, of course, is a big motivator for me."

"Hi, Mike. I didn't know if you would be up to this. How are you doing? And how are the hands?"

"My burns have healed. There is still some redness especially if they get cold. I spent a couple weeks flyfishing in the shadow of Mt. Whitney and that was the best medicine for a broken heart, but it was hell on my hands. What happened is not going to be healed and I have come to grips with that. If I can help find those responsible for

Gwynn's death and all those other innocent people, or can find out who targeted Monica and why, then I will be spending my grief in a positive direction."

McElroy was silent for a couple seconds. Mike thought the connection was lost. "Mike, I am so sorry for your loss. Your research efforts are welcome in this investigation. However, and that's with a capital H, any information you uncover must be reported immediately to me. You cannot go rogue on this. I'm working with task forces in Virginia, D.C. and Maryland on the plane bombing and we are focused on determining why Monica Linden was kidnapped. You work with me and when the case is cracked, you will have exclusive rights to the whole story. Currently, the news media has only limited information."

"That's generous of you, Agent McElroy." Mike stammered.

"Please, call me Tom."

"Okay. Tom, where are you?"

"I'm currently in the Bay Area following up on some information."

"Tom, I have some questions. Can I ask them now?"

"Yes, Sure. Shoot."

"Number one, where is Monica's body now?

"At the crime lab still. Samples collected in processing were sent to our Quantico lab, but LVMPD still has the body and duplicates of all blood and trace."

"Is it possible for us to visit the crime lab and speak to someone about their findings? I like to go to the source when possible."

"I can have that arranged. Be aware, however, the lab may have restrictions on how much they can divulge. Please remember, no publishing until case solved."

"I'll remember. Do you think Sarah and I can pay a visit tomorrow?

"Sure, I'll call over. When do you think you'll be back in the Bay Area? We can get together and I can update you. By the way, Monica's sister told me she will be planning a Life Celebration service for her sister within a few days in San Leandro. At Hope House Community Church. I plan to attend. See who shows up."

Mike made a notation of the church, "Was Monica a member of that church?"

"No, no religious affiliation or interest, according to her sister, Tanya."

"One last thing, Tom. Fill me in on the poster thing. Monica pinned up a poster on tomato genetics after checking into her room. Then she went missing. There was a switcheroo with another poster reporting on what?" Mike trailed off.

"Thermal hysteresis. It's a biological process by which

some animals keep their cells from freezing in freezing environments like Alaska or the Arctic Ocean. I don't know enough about it to say more, but there are only a handful of labs in the U.S. that conduct research on it. One such lab is at UC San Diego. A Dr. Morgan Lomax was the author and presenter of the poster next to Monica's. Monica Linden, Morgan Lomax. We're working on compiling information on his research. He is a postdoc at UCSD in a research lab headed up by Dr. Lydia Tankersley. Also, one of the keynote lectures at the conference was on antifreeze proteins. A Dr. Ricki O'Conner gave that lecture. She's with NOAA in La Jolla. Her father is an NCIS colleague of mine living in San Diego. He's flying home from Virginia to speak to his daughter and afford some protection if necessary."

"Thank you for answering all my questions. I'm sure I will have many more. Looking forward to meeting up in the Bay Area."

"Sounds good. Bye now."

The following morning, Mike and Sarah grabbed some breakfast at the hotel before checking out. Their appointment with Detective Brad Green was scheduled at 10:00. They needed to drop off Sarah's rental car on the way to the Crime Lab located in downtown Las Vegas. The morning rush hour traffic had subsided but just like in the Bay Area, traffic was heavy almost 24 hours a day. As they drove past the strip, they remarked how plain and mundane it looked. All the neon splendor and fantasy were drained from it like a whore on Sunday morning.

"Have you been to *Dreamland?*" Sarah asked.

"In sixth grade. My folks took my brother and me."

"I've been at night and I've been in the day. I wish I had never seen it during the day." Sarah said.

"'Stark' is the word that comes to mind," he said, thinking how easily color can drain from the world, leaving a grayscale scaffold of stark reality. He commenced telling Sarah about his conversation with McElroy. Sarah sucked air between her teeth when he told her about the ORNL lab in Tennessee and that two labs in San Diego were working on AFPs; one run by a Dr. Lydia Tankersley at UCSD and the other by Ricki O'Conner at NOAA.

Mike felt her tense up, "What? You know something?"

"Ricki O'Conner is a childhood friend of mine."

"What about her dad? You know him? NCIS?"

"Don? Yes. I didn't know he worked with NCIS. I thought he was retired Navy. That's how it was when we lived in Sage, OR."

"McElroy says he is working on the airplane bombing case and now this Linden case. That he's been in Quantico and flew home to San Diego this week," Mike said. Sarah got quiet and Mike could see she was upset. He understood that now they both had personal interest in the investigation. "When did you last speak to Ricki?" Mike asked.

"I dunno. Last year sometime. On the phone. We are both so absorbed in our work," her voice trailed off.

They found a parking spot at a Big-Box store two blocks from the crime lab. They stopped at the front desk and went through a security check before they were greeted by Detective Green who led them down a hallway and past the breakroom to his office. The lab was nothing like the television series. Absent was the cool, dark ambiance with blue illumination coming from wall sconces and shelf back-lighting. Instead, the halls and office were glaringly bright like you would observe in a hospital. Mike chuckled as he reflected on the previous conversation with Sarah about the Las Vegas Strip and *Dreamland – stark - like a whore on Sunday morning.*

"Agent McElroy tells me that you are good investigative reporters" Green's face was smiling but his eyes were searching for wickedness.

Mike responded, "Yes. We appreciate the opportunity to talk with you directly so that nothing is permutated or falls between the cracks. When we tell the story - and we promised to not do that until we have the green light - we want it to be one hundred percent accurate."

Sarah had her notebook out, ready to jot down every word delivered by the detective.

"Here is a summary I prepared for you. We have individual reports but, by law, I cannot give those to the public. And besides, it is difficult to wade through if you aren't familiar with the forms. Why don't you take a couple minutes to read it while I make a couple phone calls and then I'll be available to answer any questions you have." He handed them each a copy of the summary with LVMPD letterhead and escorted them to the breakroom and offered them coffee.

CASE #:
DB NVMPD ML2333078
NAME:
Monica Louise Linden
GENDER:
Female
ETHNICITY:
Caucasian
HEIGHT:
5'5
WEIGHT:
123.5 lbs
HAIR:
Brown
EYES:
Brown
ID METHOD
Dental records. Next of kin: Tanya Long, sister San Leandro, CA
DB DISCOVERY DATE:
January 22, 2012. 1504 PST
LOCATION OF DISCOVERY:

Hwy 93, 2.5 mi west of Hoover Dam.
Coordinates Lat. 36.009934, Lon. -114.766666
NDOT Construction site

SOURCE:

John Talbert (NDOT)

COD:

Single GSW to posterior cranium

DOD:

January 19, 2012 - January 21, 2012

TOD:

unknown

SEXUAL ASSAULT:

No

DEFENSE WOUNDS:

No

FINGER PRINTS:

Multiple. Construction structures. Pipe rail. Doritos package

STOMACH CONTENTS:

Grapefruit, bacon, shrimp, broccoli

TRACE:

Fingernails: none
Toes: rug fibers between toes. Hotel
Hair: linen fibers. 100% Egyptian cotton. Hotel
Genitalia: tissue fibers. Hotel

TOXICOLOGY:

Blood: Chloroform 0.001 mg/mL
Blood: Lorazepam 0.05 mg/mL
Blood: ETOH   0.021 g/dL
Liver: Chloroform 0.006 mg/mL
Liver: ETOH   0.524 mg/mL

MISCELLANEOUS:

Safety pin in pocket unique to a beauty supply store called Beautiful Thangs, 5901 Eastern Ave, Las Vegas. Partial front page Gideon Bible in the cuff of her jeans.

Sarah and Mike furiously wrote down notes and questions in their notebooks as they read the summary.

Mike had seen forensic reports before and was grateful for the time the detective took to summarize the important points. However, here there were few inferences on lab results. When Green gathered them up to his office, Mike and Sarah had many questions for him. Sarah started, "So, to be clear, Ms. Linden was held captive from the 19th until her body was found on Wednesday afternoon - the 22nd. How long before she was found was she killed?"

Green, "It is not clear. At least not at this time."

Mike, "What about the state of digestion or the alcohol blood-to-liver ratio? Can that resolve time of death?

"Unfortunately, the alcohol assays aren't helpful post-mortem because the body begins to ferment and produce ethanol on its own. As far as the stomach contents, we think she may have been killed on Tuesday sometime."

"Any insect activity that might shed light?" Mike queried.

"No, that's why we are leaning towards Tuesday. There are many uncertainties still."

Sarah, "I thought time of death was a slam dunk once you had a body. I'm surprised by these uncertainties."

"That's TV, Ma'am," Green smirked.

"Where do the prints lead?" Mike interrupted the uncomfortable moment.

"The Feds have those and are running them on larger

databases. We ruled out those that belonged to NDOT staff and construction contractors. There were a couple found on a piece of scrap metal that the Feds are interested in. We ran them in CODIS and Interpol but no matches."

"Ballistics?" Sarah chimed in, wanting Green's respect.

"No bullet, no gun, no ballistic analysis," Green shrugged his shoulders. "If we knew where she was shot, we would search for a lodged bullet. The bullet went out her left cheek adjacent the nose."

Sarah said, "Can we have images of Monica's wounds?"

Green, "Why? I don't see how that would help and I don't feel it's appropriate. You'll have to ask Mc Elroy. He has access to them."

Mike interrupted the sparring between Sarah and Det. Green, "So, what about the miscellaneous items found on Monica? Have you been able to follow up on the safety pin or the *Gideon Bible*? And why would Monica have a piece of the *Gideon Bible* in her cuff?"

"All good questions and I wish I had solid answers." Green offered. "This is what we've learned. The safety pin is supplied to only hotels that have day spas. They add the safety pins as a freebie if the hotel buys a certain amount of beauty supplies from them. Our detectives have questioned the store owners and supplied the FBI with a list of hotels that may have received these pins."

"How many hotels?" Mike interrupted. "And what precludes that Monica didn't have this pin before she went to San Diego?"

"Monica's luggage, purse, backpack – all that she traveled with, didn't come with her to Las Vegas. Thus, we assume she pocketed it while held captive."

Sarah, doing her best to not strike a defensive tone, said, "And the *Gideon Bible*? Those are fairly common in hotels, correct?"

"Not in Las Vegas, Missy," Green gloated in subliminal male dominance. "Very few, actually. People come to Las Vegas, they don't want to have a conscience."

Mike cut in, "Detective, we don't want to take up all your time. Can you tell us which hotels might have Bibles because, I agree, it's highly unlikely Monica left home with that in her cuff."

"Only West Inns. There are two in Las Vegas, one in San Diego and two in Palm Springs. The feds are running down these leads."

A chill ran up Mike's back and he stammered, "I just came from Palm Springs."

"Well, don't discount the safety pin. It's more likely the hotel we're looking for is here in Vegas."

Mike and Sarah closed their notebooks and said goodbye. Their visit took almost two hours and they were needing to get on the road. Sarah was quiet as they walked to the car, but Mike thought he could hear her swearing under her breath. He suppressed a smile.

"I think we should visit the two West Inns while we are here." Sarah said as she opened the passenger car door.

Mike agreed and asked her to look up the addresses of the two hotels. One was east at Lake Las Vegas and the other one was on the Strip. "Well, it looks like we need to go visit the Sunday Morning whore," Mike joked. Sarah laughed. They decided to go to Lake Las Vegas first.

It was a beautiful resort and they concurred had they known about it, they would have lodged there since it was off-season and per diem would cover it. Once through the lobby, they found a path that meandered through the tropical landscaping towards the beach on the Lake. Surprisingly, sunbathers were still out in force around the outdoor pool and they decided to relax and have a cocktail on the patio. Men and women dressed in formal hotel service uniforms bustled about making patrons comfortable. Mike and Sarah tried their best to blend in as a couple on vacation. Sarah started to say something about Detective Green and Mike cut her off, "Shhhhh, Sarah, let it go. There will always be people like that and you're not going to change them. He wanted to get under your skin. That's how he wins. He's a distraction." She knew he was right, but it bugged her that she wasn't able to win Green over. Alignment was an important aspect of being a successful reporter.

"Oh, I almost forgot! I need to call Ricki," Sarah said, yanking at her backpack. Ricki didn't pick up, so Sarah hung up. "I'll try again later. I don't want to leave a message. What would I say, 'Ricki, murderers are after you! Please be careful!'?"

They snacked on some appetizers, compared notes and conjectured why, when and where Monica died. It was futile given there was no primary, or bullet, or finger prints or shoeprints. Shoeprints. The summary said nothing of shoeprints. Mike made a note to ask McElroy. Suddenly, the criminal connection between whoever killed Gwynn and Monica was elusive to Mike and he realized he was tired. He was too spun up in minutia and couldn't see the big picture. He suggested that they visit the other West Inn in the morning on the way home. They each booked a room on the third floor and took refuge in their respective dens. Mike took a nap and Sarah left a message on Ricki's phone. She checked in with Fogerty and filled him in on the details of their investigation thus far. He was pleased but wanted them to finish up in Las Vegas and be back in the office by Friday. He wanted Sarah to pick up where she left off on a couple other stories, sharply stating that he still had a newspaper to run. Sarah was afraid he was moving her off the Linden case.

While riding the elevator down to meet Mike in the lounge for dinner, a man in the elevator wearing a hotel uniform began small talk with Sarah. She mentioned that she was a newspaper reporter who was looking into a case that may involve his hotel. The young man seemed enthralled that something exciting might be happening and asked enthusiastically, "What do you need to know?" The tag on his shirt was in bold print. "Emilio, I am looking for someone who may have been here early last week for a couple days. A young Caucasian woman with medium length brown hair. She possessed a safety pin that came from the spa. Does that description ring any bells?"

"No. Those safety pins many left behind by guests. Many of the rooms I clean." Emilio's English was broken somewhat but still very good. And he was not shy.

"You have Bibles in every room?"

"Si. I mean, yes. Some guest take them. Not many. I replace."

"Were you working last week? Here at the hotel. Um, the resort?"

"Si."

"Does anything stand out in your mind? Anything unusual in any room? Any guest that may have struck you strange?" He looked at her quizzically.

Sarah broke the silence, "Ah, yes, I know this is Las Vegas. I mean anything more strange than usual?"

He was feeling comfortable with her, "Si. There was a strange thing. Last week - maybe before - there was a man and a woman walking toward elevator on second floor building C. He dressed very nice, suit and tie. She not. Her shirt wrinkled like she just out of sleep. Jeans too. Cuffs rolled up had on tennis shoes. It struck me funny," said Emilio.

Sarah asked him to describe the woman. He said she had medium long hair. Not skinny. Not happy. He described the man as not big, graying hair above ears, big mustache, gap between front teeth. He had his arm locked in her arm. He smiling. She not. Emilio thought maybe they were in a fight or something. He never saw them again. He said he didn't know what room they came from. Sarah asked if there was anything else peculiar about last week. Emilio told how the carpet in one guest room had to be replaced because of a urine stain by the bed. And the wallpaper in the bathroom in the same room had to be replaced because of graffiti.

"What room and what was the graffiti?" Sarah asked.

"Someone scratched their name and date on the wall between the bathroom and shower. M.L. 1/20/2012."

Sitting across the table at dinner, Mike listened intently as Sarah described the conversation she had with Emilio. He ordered his dinner and then went to call McElroy leaving Sarah sipping on a Moscow Mule.

"Agent McElroy was grateful for your lead, Sarah. He wanted me to thank you for your skill in talking to a hotel employee and possibly identifying the primary," Mike said as he sat back down at the table. "And I didn't tell him you knew Ricki – I thought you'd want to hold off on that until you reach her."

"But I forgot to ask what room it was!" Sarah regretted.

"That's okay. Let the Federal detectives talk to Emilio. Let them take the risks, isn't that what you told me a month ago?" Mike couldn't help repeating her words back to her.

It was already Wednesday and Fogerty insisted they be back in the office Friday morning. They checked out and headed north on the 515 until it turned into Hwy 95. Neither felt it was necessary anymore to check out the West Inn on The Strip and were happy to leave Las Vegas. At Scotty's Junction they headed west across Death Valley. Mike had been wondering if Sarah would mind if he threw a line in the river one more time before he went back to his life in San Francisco. The memories he had of casting his fly line out high over the river and watching it being carried by convection until it landed softly upstream in the feeding lane, hung like a blessed veil between heaven and the human condition. A large thunderhead hung in the sky to the west as they drove through Death Valley and he wondered if it was going to prohibit fishing. *One typically does not stick a graphite rod in the air during a lightning storm.* When they hit Hwy 395, they turned north until they were in Lone Pine where they grabbed some sandwiches to go. Mike headed to a section of the Owens River where he had had luck a couple weeks ago and they sat on the bank to eat.

"Mike," Sarah said. "I'm afraid Fogerty is thinking about taking me off the story. He said he needed me back and had a newspaper to run."

Mike was quiet for a minute, remembering what Fogerty said about the lead. "I may have established rapport with an FBI agent, but you have a long-established relationship not only with an antifreeze protein researcher but also an NCIS investigator. I don't think he will take you off the story once he knows that. Did Ricki O'Conner ever call back?"

"No," Sarah moaned. "I'll try again when you are fishing."

13 Convergence

Mike aimed for a feeding lane, using one of the BWO parachute flies that Fred had sold him earlier that month. It was colder than it had been on his previous visit and blue winged olives weren't working. He tied on a pale morning dun and that was equally unsuccessful. He switched to a *Caddis* nymph and tried the roll-cast-and-high-sticking technique. Sarah got so excited when he caught his first fish that she forgot about calling Ricki. She was mesmerized by the sun's reflection off the moving water and remembered fishing diamond-studded lake water back home when she was young. She felt pangs of homesickness, trying to recall the last time she visited her parents in Sage. Two hours had passed since lunch and it was starting to get cold. She called Ricki and this time Ricki picked up.

"Well, hello old friend," Sarah said, looking off toward

the mountains.

"Hi Sarah. Who you callin' old, *B*? I saw you've called several times. I just haven't had time to return your call. How are you? Where are you? I hear running water and wind."

Sarah said, "I'm on the Owens River with a colleague, flyfishing. It's beautiful but cold and windy. And my city clothes are not up to the elements."

"The *Inquisitor* pays you to go fishing these days?" Ricki poked fun at Sarah.

"No. I mean, yes. I'm not fishing but he is. We're on our way back to San Francisco from Las Vegas. We're on a story.

"What's his name and are you…?"

"No, no. Nothing like that," Sarah interrupted. "Mike? We're just friends. He lost his fiancée just a couple months ago. He is working on getting through it. The story we're on involves her death. She was on the plane that..." Sarah stopped short to avoid going into details. "Actually, Ricki, I just learned that this story involves you, and your research, and I wanted to warn you."

Ricki was silent and then said, "You're working on the Monica Linden case, aren't you? How did you get involved?"

Sarah was caught off guard but jumped to the point,

"Yes. You and Lydia Tankersley are both targets in what appears to be an international industrial espionage caper."

"I knew Linden had been kidnapped from FFG but I assumed it was random. There was some speculation that an adjacent poster was implicated…" Ricki paused. "So how is it you got involved? That's so weird."

Sarah jumped into the tense moment with a monolog, "We are working with an FBI agent. Mike met him after Gwynn died. We are under strict orders to report only to him, so I am reluctant to divulge any information. This agent and your dad are both working the case. That's how I found out you are in danger. I doubt Don knows we know Agent McElroy. The two of them need to talk so we can all be on the same page."

"My dad will be home today. He sounded distant. Now I know why. How did Gwynn die?"

Sarah hesitated on disclosing information but wanted Ricki to know the extent of danger, "The recent plane bombing at SFO"

There was notable silence in Ricki before she muttered, "Oh, shit."

By the time they were back in the car and heading north on 395, it was already 5:30. Since they didn't have to meet with Fogerty until Friday morning, they decided to get lodging in Bridgeport. Most of the passes through the

Sierra Nevada Mountains were still closed for the winter. Only Carson, Echo and Donner were open, and Carson was the closest. They would set out in the early morning and be home by early afternoon. Mike called McElroy and told him about Sarah knowing Don and Ricki. He was surprised by the connection and said he would call Don later that night. McElroy said that Emilio and the West Inn in Lake Las Vegas checked out. There was tangible evidence that Monica was there. The carpet wasn't found, the wallpaper with her initials and date had been replaced but management took photos for insurance purposes. The room had been occupied by several guests since the repairs, but fingerprints were lifted anyway. Employees have been screened and they are currently running guest fingerprints. A suite of fingerprints near the window was a positive match to Monica's. Tom said that the room was thoroughly tested for blood trace, but none was found, meaning that the primary crime scene remains unidentified. Mike shared this information with Sarah over dinner at their hotel in Bridgeport. She took notes on her phone.

They made small talk - if they talked at all - as they drove through the mountains and across the valley. The mountains made Sarah miss home and she made a note in her phone to visit her parents soon. They both were fatigued and looked forward to sleeping in their own beds. As they came over the San Mateo Bridge towards SFO, Mike began to sweat. Sarah's car was parked at the airport and she needed to be dropped off there. He asked if she would be alright as he dropped her off at the parking lot entrance. She nodded yes and made her way to her car and then to her flat in Daly City. Mike slept very little that night, despite the comfort of his own bed and familiar sounds. What sleep did come was peppered with dreams of fishing with his dad and brother in the Ozarks intermingled, disturbingly, with memories of Gwynn and the violence of the blast. His three and a half weeks on the road felt like a year in many ways and the blast at the airport felt like a scene from a movie.

14 Precocious Children ❧

Don boarded the plane with one suitcase and a briefcase. Once seated, he began to joke with other Space A flight passengers, knowing that after take-off, everyone would try to sleep through the eight-hour flight from Quantico to San Diego. Some were returning to their home base after specialized training, some were just returning home. Don, for the first time since Monterey, was worried about Ricki. He didn't know what to tell her, or more accurately, how much *not* to tell her. Though a grown woman now, he still imagined that he could control her fate and keep her safe. He had promised his wife, Anne, that he would. Anne felt like she was letting Ricki down by dying - that she was abandoning her. The guilt over not successfully birthing Ricki's older brother provided a scaffold that attracted guilt. She wanted to name him Richard after her father, but when the baby boy died at three hours old after bleeding to death in her arms from what the doctor called fetomaternal hemorrhaging, she agreed to name him John after Don's dad. The gravestone read: "John Ellerman O'Conner, In the Arms of Angels, May 9, 1974 - May 9, 1974". Despite her strong faith in God's benevolence, she was fearful throughout her second pregnancy. But, the second delivery was perfect, as was her baby. Holding her newborn baby girl in her arms, she grinned at Don and said, "I know we agreed to name her Sarah, but I really believe her name is Ricki." Don was so relieved to have a healthy baby and wife that he would have agreed with any name she picked, even if it sounded like a boy's name. And now their baby daughter was in danger simply because she chose to conduct research on a biochemical that businessmen would kill for. How could he tell Ricki to change her research interests? Or forfeit established grant agreements and collaborations? As long as the perps were at large, she would be a target. They already ransacked the ORNL lab at the University of Tennessee looking for possible patent applications. They had names of every person that had worked in the Molecular Biophysics lab in the last seven years. Agent McElroy had said that only a few U. S. labs were working on thermal hysteresis and Ricki's was one of them.

When Ricki arrived home, Don was sitting in his recliner watching the news. He got up and awkwardly embraced her and they made small talk about his plane ride, where they might go to eat dinner. Behind the small talk was a sense of expectancy and anxiety. Ricki wanted to order take out, but Don wanted to go out knowing that their domicile might be wired. He wanted freedom to talk to his daughter as he sought fit without snooping ears. They decided on a popular pizza joint, populated with college and high school kids. They ordered a combination pizza and found a table outside where they could talk. Before Don began, Ricki said, "Sarah's involved."

Don's blank look told Ricki that he didn't already know. Agent Mc Elroy didn't tell him. "She called me to warn me that I might be in danger because of my research and that she and a journalist colleague are working with an FBI agent named McElroy. She didn't want to tell me much until I talked with you. She knows you are working on the Linden case with McElroy. I know that the SFO bombing is somehow implicated in Linden's kidnapping and murder. That's about all I know. Oh, and the colleague she is working with? His fiancée was killed in the SFO blast. His name is Mike. I don't know his last name. He likes to fly fish. Oh, and there are agents watching over me and Lydia Tankersley."

Don's head was cocked to one side and his mouth was open as he took in all she said. Now he had to rearrange his strategy and method of telling Ricki what she needed to know.   She knew almost everything. Ricki's smooth strawberry blond hair draped halfway over her face as she fiddled with the napkin in front of her, eyes cast down like a child waiting for a verdict after confessing an infraction.

"Ricki, I wasn't going to tell you much, but that's blown all to hell." Don leaned back in the chair, displaying annoyance. "I'll need to contact Tom and let him know about the connection between us and Sarah."

"He probably already knows. Sarah and Mike were going to tell him this evening. They were on their way back to the Bay Area from Las Vegas when Sarah called me. She didn't tell me many details because of their agreement with the agent."

"She told you plenty!" Don's face red and tense. "Much more than I was planning on telling you. Yes, you are in danger and the less you know, the safer you will be. There are agents tailing you and Dr. Tankersley. In fact, there is probably one outside right now and one still at our Townhouse. Someone has already interviewed Dr. Tankersley but I wanted to be the one to interview you."

Ricki told him the extent of her research and how she gave the Keynote Lecture at FFG for Lydia and that a postdoc, Morgan Lomax, presented a poster. Don told her how Lomax had put his poster up in Linden's assigned space and investigators believe that is the reason she was abducted. He also told her how a small international oil company based in Canada was suspected of hacking a large American oil company name Rangor, Incorporated. Rangor, Inc. was funding some research at ORNL on antifreeze proteins. "The lab at ORNL was ransacked and then set on fire. The fire was quickly extinguished and we were able to collect some evidence. A couple of suspects are in custody." Don also said that whoever targeted the ORNL lab is suspected in both the Linden case and, also, the SFO bombing. He didn't tell her that the perps have a list of people that worked in the ORNL Center of Molecular Biophysics lab where Ricki had been a postdoc.

Ricki interjected, "I thought Neptune was responsible for the SFO bombing."

"No, that was sloppy reporting. Turns out Neptune has left its activist ways in the past, is now a non-profit organization that provides educational services, agreements and grants supporting marine ecology. Neptune has provided us with a list of names that left the organization because they believed Neptune was selling out to capitalist pigs. We are following up on those individuals - criminal records, IRS files, DNA profiles, genealogy companies, surveillance, etc. All of this takes time. We don't know if they dispersed or formed a currently operating cell. Neptune went public four and a half years ago. We know that there was an executive from Rangor, Inc. on flight 1561 to New York who may have been the target. Ironically, his assigned seat was across the aisle from Mike's fiancée. We recovered some material from a briefcase located a few hundred yards from the wreckage. It contained information about thermal hysteresis in mammals. Whoever perpetrated the bombing of Flight 1561 is most likely also responsible for the ORNL lab and murdering the Linden woman. We just need to connect the dots."

Ricki picked at her pizza. Her appetite had waned after hearing her dad throw out so many diabolic dots. She didn't believe that she, herself, was in much danger but that Lydia, who had worked on hysteresis for many years, was. Her postdoc's poster was on antifreeze proteins in mice. She agreed Morgan was the target, not Monica.

15 Standing Your Ground ◦

Lydia dropped Shara off at school as usual, making sure she stayed within the lane for quick drop off. One way to turn a good morning bad was to disobey the traffic volunteer who coordinated student drop-off. She didn't know the woman's name and didn't want to. She focused on getting through the task of dropping Shara off without interaction with this woman. Just the shrill of her voice could make needles crawl from your ears to your toes. After getting settled at her desk, Lydia listened to her voicemails while fiddling with a plastic DNA model. She returned Ricki's call. "Hey, Ricki. Returning your call."

"Yeah, hi Lydia. How are you doing? I have something to discuss with you, pertaining to Monica Linden. The woman kidnapped at FFG?"

"Yes, I remember," Lydia said abruptly.

"My dad came home. He works in law enforcement and Homeland Security stuff, most of which I am kept completely in the dark about. But he flew home from Quantico yesterday concerned about my research - our research - in AFPs. That includes you and Morgan."

Lydia replied, "The FBI interviewed me a couple days ago. They said that the Linden woman's body was found. They wanted to know where Morgan was and I told them he was on vacation in Mexico. They asked my whereabouts last week and why I didn't go to the conference. I told them I skipped the conference because it had gotten old and I took my daughter to visit her dad in Las Vegas for the weekend. They knew who Carl was, and where he lived, which freaked me out."

"You were in Las Vegas last weekend? You're jesting, right? That's where Monica Linden's body was found. She was murdered. Did you stay in Las Vegas the whole weekend or did you drive home after dropping off your daughter?"

Lydia was feeling uncomfortable with the way Ricki was grilling her. "Like I told the authorities, I stayed at the West Inn Resort at Lake Las Vegas Friday afternoon until Tuesday afternoon before picking up Shara and driving home. They have all that information."

Ricki sensed the change in Lydia's tone so she changed the subject. Everyone that ever worked in Lydia's lab had

had the experience of finding themselves in her crosshairs once she got riled. Anyone with any instinct whatsoever kept on their toes. Ricki remembered the time a grad student did a rotation in the lab. He was brilliant but was affected with Asperger Syndrome and had trouble reading non-verbal language. Not being able to read Lydia's non-verbal language was like being a bird in a cage with a cat. "Lydia, my dad said we have people watching out for us, but please, be careful and keep eyes in the back of your head. The lab I worked in at ORNL was hacked and then burned."

"I'm not going to stop doing research. They need to catch the bad guys so we can do our jobs. What the hell do I pay taxes for?" Lydia was riled, signaling Ricki it was time to hang up. Mid-morning, Lydia ambled to the coffee cart in front of Mink Hall and noticed that two men who didn't look like students were sitting on a bench facing the sculpture of a giant eye. One had short graying hair, the other long scraggly hair and a beard. She surmised that they were undercover agents spying on her. She silently crop-dusted them as she walked past them on the way back to her building. At noon, she noticed them again in the Student Union courtyard. They were sitting 15 meters apart, one on a bench and the other at a table. She did not like being under surveillance, even if they were there to protect her. She walked by the one on the bench and purposefully let the plastic fork slip from her hand. A woman sitting on the same bench picked it up and handed it to her with a cordial smile.

16 Sliding Doors ❧

Don drove Ricki to work Thursday morning. He asked her to not ride her bike anymore but to drive her car or let him take her. Life at the lab was comforting to her where she could believe that nothing had changed. She went through her routine like always, discussing projects with various lab members and returning phone calls. One call was to Lydia who didn't pick up and so began the game of phone tag. She went on Lydia's staff page and looked at the scope of research her lab was doing on AFPs. She was surprised to discover that she had launched some recent projects in collaboration with the Center of Molecular Biophysics lab at ORNL on thermal hysteresis in primates. CMB always worked toward an economical outcome so Ricki searched until she found the treasured nugget. *Prevention of Frostbite*: How to extend application from prevention of freezer burn in ice cream and damage to ovaries in cryogenic reproduction therapy to prevention of freezer burn in live corneas, fingers and toes. She could see how a Canadian oil company would want to harness the ability to prevent frostbite during long exposure to the elements in oil sands mining or expanding operations north into the Arctic Basin. She could also see why ecologists would oppose both sands oil extraction and drilling in pristine arctic environments, given the toxic by-products produced and habitat destruction. Don had explained to her that the fingerprints found at the ORNL lab belonged to an ex-member of Neptune who drifted from the organization seven years ago. He was a 44-year-old high school dropout arrested in 2002 for shoplifting at a SmartMart store in Arizona. He had been on a watchlist the last six years suspected of involvement with a loosely organized mercenary group that contracted out for various assignments.

Staring absently at her monitor, Ricki pondered who posed the most danger: *an oil company driven by greed and desperately trying to outrace its competitors, or eco-freaks committing heinous crimes of violence to champion their cause. Homocentric obsession came in many flavors. Whether it's simply greed for money and power, or a dire emotional need to keep the world exactly as is, it's all man-focused. And narcissistic.* Her mother's words seeped into her consciousness, *'From whence come wars and fightings among you? Come they not from your lusts that war in your members?*

You lust and do not have. You murder and covet and cannot obtain. You fight and war. Yet you do not have because you do not ask. You ask and do not receive, because you ask amiss, that you may spend it on your pleasures.' It baffled her how these passages seemed to come out of nowhere like bubbles from the benthos.

Ricki bundled up and went out to the open area west of the lab to eat lunch and sat facing the ocean. Before she opened her bag of fruit and nuts, she walked to the edge of the bluff to look down. The waves weren't particularly big, but the cool breeze amplified the sound of the waves crashing on the rocks below so that they sounded like thunder rolling across the landscape. The water was clear indicating significant upwelling. She thought, *the Pacific was displaying its finest glory today,* but she instinctively backed away from the edge as her vision constricted and she felt a rush of adrenaline flood her senses. She was content gazing at the vessel-dotted horizon while she ate her lunch, her mind preoccupied with many questions, foremost, why she took the reductionist path in her career, studying molecules. She wondered, humoring herself, if it was too late to join the Coast Guard.

17 Home Turf

The meeting with Fogerty on Friday morning went well. At least for Mike. He was to continue working closely with the FBI. Sarah was right in thinking that Fogerty was diverting her energy toward other stories. He agreed that since she was close friends with Ricki and her family, that she remain loosely involved in the case. Sarah knew and trusted Mike well enough to know that he would keep her in the loop. She returned to routine work in her cubicle for most of Friday and called her parents before booking a flight to Oregon. She rode the train home and packed for the weekend, declining an invitation from some friends to join them at a nearby restaurant. Before she went to bed, she received a phone text from Ricki inviting her to San Diego. She received a second message from Don, asking if she would mind visiting with Ricki. He needed to be out of town for a couple days and felt uncomfortable leaving her alone. She called her parents and said she was sorry she had to disappoint them. They agreed with her choice to comply with Don's wishes. She told them she thought they were awesome and that she would be up to visit them as soon as she could. She changed her flight destination from Salem to San Diego and repacked for a milder climate.

Mike called Sarah in the morning and left a voice message saying that Monica's memorial service was that day and asked if she wanted to attend. He felt guilty about Fogerty's directive that he would proceed on the story without her. But Fogerty was right in that the story was slow in developing and until the authorities cracked the case, nothing tangible could benefit the newspaper. There was always the danger that unscrupulous carnivorous journalists would scoop the story, even if what they reported were quarter-truths. But if they were to keep the respect of the FBI, they would sit on the story until it became ripe. He made certain to explain in the voicemail to Sarah that McElroy had called Mike about Monica's service late Friday evening. After the service, they planned to have lunch and discuss findings. He was somewhat glad that his call went to voicemail.

18 Musky Business

Friday morning came as usual, another work week gone. Morgan would be gone yet another week. After what Ricki said the day before, she was glad he was safely squirreled away from the lab. Lydia managed to drop Shara off without engaging the mom-micro-manager-from-hell. She rerouted to work in order to pick up a Latte at a drive-thru and avoid the coffee cart at Mink Hall. Parking was a pain. Stopping to get coffee made her arrive after class had started, which meant a scarcity of parking spots. She had to park a block away in Lot C. Loaded up with purse, laptop, and coffee she leaned into the car to push the lock button on the door console. When she straightened up to close the door, she felt a hand over her mouth and nose and an arm around the front of her throat, dragging her backwards. Before being shoved through a car door, she heard a woman's voice say, "watch her head". Before losing consciousness, she caught a glimpse of a beard and tangled hair and the smell of musk.

19 Book Ends ❧

Ricki picked up Sarah at the airport and they stopped for breakfast in La Jolla. It had been over two years since they saw each other. Sarah still looked like Ricki remembered her - soft and approachable. "Sarah, I'm surprised you haven't hooked up with someone yet. You are gorgeous and still so grounded."

"I dunno, I like living alone. It gives me time to do what's important to me." Sarah replied.

"And what's that?"

"Read a book, do yoga, take walks, sit on the beach, hang out with friends, work when I want. My friends who are married don't have those choices. They need to coordinate everything with their mate and visa versa. At least that seems the way it works. I guess if I found someone that knocked me off my feet, I would make that adjustment. I just haven't."

"What about this Mike guy? Your coworker?" Ricki looking over the rim of her cup of coffee.

"No, no, no - no. You don't understand. We are colleagues and besides, he just lost his fiancée. In the plane bombing at SFO a couple months ago. He was there putting his long-time girlfriend on the plane. He was badly injured, she died."

"Oh, wow! You didn't tell me that. That's horrible. How is he doing?"

"Yeah, I told you his fiancée died. His burns are healing. He's trying to cope. He took time off work to travel but then this Monica Linden case came up and our boss wanted him on the story. You know the rest. What about you?" Sarah shifting focus to Ricki's single state.

"Oh my God. Where do I start? You know about Steve already. Well, that kinda did it for me. I saw how easily I was pulled off course - '*derailed*' as my dad would say. I've worked too hard for too long to throw it all away. I'm like you though - if I found someone I just couldn't live without, I might consider a committed relationship again." Ricki moaned, "I live with my dad, Sarah. I struggle with that and I'm sure any prospective mate would also!"

"Oh, come on, Ricki. Don respects your adulthood, doesn't he? I mean you even call him Don half the time.

And he's gone quite a bit, isn't he? By the way, when did he start working investigations again?"

"I found out he never stopped. Even when we lived in Sage, he was still working cases. Contractual. When I became embedded in research at UCSD and then landed this job at NOAA, he relocated here and amped up his work again. He's in Virginia half the time."

"He's a good dad, Ricki. He did a remarkable job raising you after your mom passed. Really. You are a lucky girl."

"How are your parents?" Ricki quickly shifting focus back to Sarah.

"They're good. Mom has arthritis pretty bad and stays home most of the time. She loves to cook and dad runs to the store to grab any ingredient she might need. He loves her cooking. They live in the same house – so far, anyway. I don't know how long that will last. I need to get up there and visit them. It's been a while and I feel bad about that. Work seems to monopolize my time. I know they are proud of me, but I hear sadness in their voices over the phone – lamentation. I don't call as often as I should because what I think will be a 10-minute howdy doody check-in becomes a 40-minute monolog about the neighbor's cat, or nephew, or the nephew's cat, or some tangential thing like that. It's frustrating. I only want to hear about them! I think they think that because I wrote for the paper in Sage that I am interested in all that local gossip. I am so not." Sarah stopped talking as she felt her frustration rise.

Ricki absorbed Sarah's angst and capitulated the conversation with, "We have very different realities regarding parents, don't we?"

20 Darkness, My Old Friend

Lydia's heart began to race as she realized that her hands were bound behind her. Her head ached and her vision was blurred. Her neck hurt as she slowly raised her head off her chest. She didn't know how long she had been out but remembered some ugly-assed guy doping her and shoving her into the back seat of a car in the C lot. She tried to manage her rage as panic rushed up her throat. She was in a chair in the corner of a room darkened by wainscoted walls. She saw faint light coming through gingham curtains covering a window on a door to her right. There was a table near the far wall with a coffee maker, some Hostess Ho Hos, a handgun, her purse, laptop and cell phone on top. She heard faint snoring but couldn't see its source. She wiggled her wrists trying to see if she could loosen her bonds. She became determined to get free when she discovered that ropey material was holding her wrists. She knew if she ever wanted to see her daughter again, she had to get free - and soon. It wasn't rocket science to figure out these were the same people who killed Monica. She wondered about Morgan, if he was okay south of the border. Her hands eventually loosened the knot in the twine. She stuffed it up her sleeve so it wouldn't fall to the floor. There was a figure slumped in an overstuffed chair in the corner to the left of the table and a cracked door in the far corner. It took too long to untie the rope around her feet and she shoved down fatalist thoughts that her window for escape would abruptly end. She busied her mind assessing the room, planning her next move. The gingham-clad door to the outside seemed like the best choice but she didn't know if it was key-locked or latched from the inside. She tried to see the door knob, but it was obscured by a broom handle leaning up against the wall. Finally, free, she shifted her weight in the wood chair and was pleased it made no sound. The snoring continued its rhythm. She slowly stood up and her weight made the floor creak. Adrenaline rocketed up her spine and she reached with both arms for the gun and cell phone before bolting for the door. The man jolted up, confused. She reached the door and twisted the deadbolt lever. She turned when she felt the man's hulk coming upon her back and smacked his head as hard as she could with the barrel of the gun. He fell backward and she ran out the door into a wooded landscape. She ran into darkness, praying she didn't trip or fall as the lights came on in the fenestrated cabin behind her. She heard a woman's voice angrily shriek something and then a single gunshot. Lydia's adrenalin kicked into a higher gear and she began to run like a cougar, using all four limbs to hop over obstacles that populated her trajected path. Her pupils were already adjusted for darkness and she could see very well. She saw a ravine, still dark in the shadow of night, and quietly made her way toward it, hiding behind Coulter pines and boulders. She couldn't tell if she was still being followed or not. Her breathing was too loud. Descending into the ravine, she stopped for a moment to listen and assess. She discovered the safety on the gun was off and was grateful she hadn't shot herself when she clobbered *Ugly*. She checked her cell phone's reception and battery level, then muted it. After holding her breath and listening for a good minute, she crawled into an undercut bank and opened a birding app designed for snapping photos and recording location. She took a picture of her feet and the gun, held the phone out under the sky and uploaded it with a text message to Ricki. She could see that the sun was ascending upstream of the ravine which meant the coast was downstream. She didn't know whether to stay hidden and wait for help or try to find her way to a road or house. Having the gun gave her confidence and she decided to move.

21 Beaches

The short drive from the cafe to Ricki's Townhouse in La Jolla was quiet with Sarah rubber-necking the whole way. Sarah noticed the dark SUV a half block away, following them, but didn't say anything to Ricki. She was comforted by the tail McElroy assigned, but wasn't sure Ricki shared her sentiment. The morning fog had burned off early and Ricki suggested they walk down to the beach. She had access to the Scripps pier which jutted into the Pacific. Migrating whales sometimes came in close to shore and watching them would be a relaxing way to spend the day. The other option would be to go to the Birch Aquarium which was within walking distance, whatever Sarah felt like. Sarah preferred the pier idea, so they packed up some snacks and headed for the beach. It was still early and the beach was fairly unoccupied. Its length stretched from La Jolla cove to the cliffs north of the NOAA facility. Beyond that lie expensive homes, a golf-course and the

Torrey Pines Reserve. The wind waves hadn't picked up yet and the tide was out so talking was easy as they meandered along the water line, picking up interesting relics tossed up in the night.

"Sarah, do you ever think about how you came to this place in life? Are you happy with your position, where you live, your friends?"

Sarah thought about it and said, "I guess I don't think about it. I still think I am in transition. I mean I've been at the same newspaper for six years but that isn't like a lifetime or anything. I'm still open for the next thing. As far as my friends? I have a small social network outside of work. We go hiking, kayaking and out for dinner on weekends. I'm not sure I could call any of them 'two-in-the-morning friends'. I think if I had to call anyone at two in the morning, it would be my colleague, Mike. It's the nature of our work. I know he has my back."

"Hey *B*, you could call me." Ricki grabbed Sarah's elbow and spun her around. They both laughed and then continued scanning the sand. Ricki stopped and pointed to the horizon. There was a pod of dolphins swimming south just beyond wave break. She gave her binoculars to Sarah to have a look. Sarah pointed to the north and said, "Spouts!". Ricki looked just in time to see the fluke of a humpback whale descend. They watched quietly, and, in the moment, time fell off their shoulders like a mantle and they were teens again.

Ricki pointed out all the various Scripps buildings as they walked and asked if Sarah cared to see her lab at NOAA. Sarah declined, saying she would rather stay outside, and that Ricki could tell her about AFP research when they were on the pier. They found a sunny spot at the end of the pier sheltered from the breeze where they could continue to talk. "So, I'm curious about this Mike guy. How old is he and what is his background?" Ricki asked while nonchalantly biting into a red apple.

"He's about 41 – somewhere around there. He's a good journalist who grew up in the south, the Ozark Mountains of southern Missouri if I remember correctly. And he just lost his lady. Tragically. They met when they were teens. He's damaged." Sarah eyed Ricki as she continued to ask about him.

"If they've been together that long, why aren't they married, etc. etc.?"

"I don't know really. He says it's because she is – was - very independent. She was a successful business attorney in Manhattan who was not quite ready to cash in her career for love and family."

Ricki sighed, "My hat goes off to her there. I forsook my life's dream for that postdoc, Steve. It was like I was on tractor beams or hypnotized or something. I couldn't see my hand in front of my face let alone my future. *"Derailed I was,"* she said in her best sci-fi voice. In a more genuine tone she said, "I can't imagine losing someone that way. He must be a train wreck. Don't you think it odd that the FBI would want him so close to the case?"

"I hadn't really thought about it. Our employer asked me to initiate the investigation and to see if Mike wanted involvement. He balked at first but then we both got caught up in the Linden story. What did Don say about Mike?"

"He didn't say anything. He pretty well keeps me on a need-to-know basis. I know he is sworn to secrecy and that he wants to protect me but sometimes he makes me nuts. You remember how he was in Sage? He was working cases then and I didn't even know it. And remember that time on the bluff? The boat? I still don't know what that was about, though I have asked on several occasions. Need-to-know basis." Ricki was clearly getting peeved, so Sarah changed the subject. She asked about the Torrey Pines Reserve and said that she might be writing an article on the natural history of the endangered tree.

Ricki said, "The newspapers here in SoCal have covered the topic fairly thoroughly. But I can link you up with someone involved in conservation efforts if that's something that will help."

"In a nutshell, why are the pines dying?" Sarah asked.

"No nutshell about it. It depends on who you ask. At first, it was because of pitch canker, a fungal pathogen. Then they said it was because of drought. But that wasn't a plausible correlation because there was also mortality on the irrigated golf course nearby. Then beetle infestation. Now, there are conjectures that it might be aluminum in the fog."

"What?"

"Yeah. Vaporized aluminum. I don't think people know why the trees are disappearing. Torrey Pine only exists here in this locale and on Santa Rosa, an island right out there," Ricki said pointing north toward the Channel Islands.

"I think I would like to take you up on that contact. Do you think I could visit the island?"

"No problemo. It makes for a great day trip," Ricki replied. "I think we should go home soon. I just realized I don't have my phone and Don asked me to check in regularly. Dads these days…" She shrugged her shoulders and Sarah responded in kind, grinning. Ricki added, "I'd like to show you the aquarium later this afternoon or we could go see the Torrey Pine Reserve."

"Yeah, either one. We could do the Reserve tomorrow. My flight isn't until 6:45."

22 Covert Farewell

The church in San Leandro was small. Agent McElroy and Mike arrived at different times and shook hands, posing as a dad and son, uncle and cousin to Monica. McElroy greeted Monica's sister, Tanya, with a cheek kiss and expressed his sympathy. She expressed gratefulness for his support and referred to him as Uncle Thomas, according to their prearranged agreement. Don arrived by taxi from the Oakland Airport and remained aloof, sitting alone near the back of the church. The service was typical, with pictures of Monica and Tanya as children, pictures of their parents and grandparents, of high school graduation – all the pictures that are customary at a celebration of life service. No casket. Monica's body was still in Las Vegas. Tanya had arranged for it to be cremated after it was released. A minister began talking about life and loved ones and the fragility of life, about death and the afterlife. He lamented that Monica's life had ended too soon and of a violent nature. Tanya cried as he spoke of unbelief and its hold on our society, "robbing God's children of a rich and fulfilling life". There were very few people in attendance. Mostly young people dressed in blue jeans, white socks and suede sandals. Don assumed most were coworkers. He snapped photos of the back of their heads and their positions in the church. Uncle Thomas and his son, Mike, sat eight rows from the front and took pictures of various people as they stood up to share their memories of Monica. As funeral goers regaled the attributes of the late Monica, there were the usual tears that accompany a close brush with mortality. None seemed remarkable. It appeared that Monica was an introvert who mostly kept to herself but was respected as a geneticist.

The service was short and afterward there was milling outside. A distinct gaggle of sandal-donners, clearly ARS co-workers, mingled near the steps. There was an agent in an unmarked vehicle, one house down and across the street, taking photos of everyone coming from the church. Don leaned against the railing, smiling and making nice with people passing by. A few shook hands with him and started small talk. Most belonged to the church, trying to make him feel welcome. When they asked how he knew Monica, he told them he had Monica as a student years ago at UC Berkeley. Thankfully, none asked him what department except one slightly older man who could have also been a professor of hers. He wore a golf shirt, too-long slacks and a herringbone sports jacket. He had an easy-going, friendly way about him and seemed to have affection for Monica. He shook his head after sipping punch from a plastic cup, saying in a thick French accent, "Such a waste." Don asked him how he knew Monica and he said he knew her from international conferences, that his name was John, a geneticist from Quebec. Don shifted his position to the left so that John was facing the agent sitting in the car, snapping photos. Don held out his hand for a cordial good-bye handshake. John reciprocated the farewell and stepped into the church foyer toward the bathroom. The crowd eventually dispersed, and Uncle Thomas and Mike said their good-byes to Tanya and her husband.

Mike, Tom and Don changed into casual clothes before leaving the church and took Mike's car to a spacious pizza joint on Bay Farm Island. They had a table in the corner where they could talk without being overheard. The restaurant was starting to fill up with pubescent sweaty soccer players and their parents. Mike had his notebook out as Tom started going over leads, "The arrest at NCBI in Maryland was turning out to be very fruitful…" Tom didn't get very far before Mike interrupted.

"What arrest at NCBI? What is NCBI?"

"There was an assault on the security guard at the NCBI

– National Center Biotechnical Institute. The perp, Mason Bailey, age 44, is talking. He has advanced liver disease and was persuaded to cooperate in exchange for a transplant. He has adult children that will visit him in prison. It's the first promising lead we've had on getting to the bottom of this thing. His prints were also found at the ORNL lab, so we know he is connected to the Linden abduction. We know there is some connection between the SFO bombing and the Linden case - we just don't know how exactly, other than interest in antifreeze proteins."

Don added, "We know that a mercenary firm recruits disenfranchised eco-terrorists - or anyone for that matter - for espionage, kidnapping, drug smuggling, blackmail, murder, assassinations, you name it. It can be a source of funding for terrorist cells planning their independent activities. We suspect a struggling oil company from Manitoba, Zimri Oil, Incorporated, may have interest in obtaining patent rights to antifreeze technology ahead of larger, well-funded oil companies like Rangor. Mr. Auckman from Rangor Oil was likely an eco-terrorist target because of the threat posed to northern habitats by expanded exploration, mining and drilling. The NGO, Neptune, has been helpful in explaining resistance to arctic oil harvesting as well as identifying possible persons of interest."

Mike objected, "That doesn't make sense to me. How

could an ecologically-minded person be hired to facilitate plans to exploit the very landscape he's committed to protect. How does he take that money and use it to resist, or destroy, the very economic machinery that just employed him? It's ludicrous."

Tom responded, "Often there is a huge disconnect in the minds of these kind of individuals. Some are schizophrenic or have some sort of psychosis. Most aren't dealing with a full deck after years – decades – of alcohol or drug abuse. They do not see the discrepancy between their actions and values."

"That's pretty crazy," Mike said. "What about the fingerprints found where Monica's body was dumped?"

"So far, there are no matches for the partial prints lifted at the site" Tom said. "Right now, the church is being dusted for prints and Don was able to retrieve a cup disposed in the men's bathroom. Don, tell us about the Canadian geneticist you met."

Don recounted his encounter with the graying mustached man with a French accent. The photos taken at the church had already been uploaded onto the FBI server. There were two persons of interest and the French man was one of them. The other was a male sitting in row five near the wall. He appeared to not know others and left right after the service was over. Tom brought up his picture on the laptop. The agent in the car did a good job getting several angles of this individual as he entered and left the church. Evidently, there was something about this guy that flagged the agent in the car. Face recognition was a positive match for a 33-year-old man from Arcata, CA named Reginald Bussey, Jr. He has an undergraduate degree in marine ecology but never found work in his field. He grew marijuana in the Emerald Triangle for a living and was a supporter of Neptune before it went 501c. He was arrested in Mendocino County for DUI in 2002 and for petty theft in 2007."

"And my French friend?" queried Don.

"Jean-Marc Rousseau according to Interpol. Age 58. Citizen of Quebec. MBA from Concordia University Montreal. Has a Financial Consulting Firm in Ottawa, travels a lot."

Don interrupted, "So not a geneticist?"

Tom replied, "Not even remotely."

Don and Mike were silent as the gravity of identifying a major player of the mercenary group sunk in. Don broke the pensive silence, "So why go to the dead woman's funeral? Why expose himself to the risk?"

"Good question. When we catch the sonovobitch, we'll ask him," Tom grinned.

23 Stealth is Wealth ✺

Lydia picked her way along the bottom of the ravine until she heard a noise coming from the north. There was an outcropping that partly hid her ascent out of the ravine on the south bank where she hid behind a clump of trees. Daylight was stalled in the shadows, giving her a dark place to hide. She took another picture of herself and sent it to Ricki adding the text, "Help! Hurry!" She knew it would take forever to send a message under the canopy of trees, so she started to move out toward a clearing toward the west. Without warning, she felt an arm around her neck and a blunt jab in her back. In that terrifying moment, her mind saw Shara, young and defenseless and begging for help. Her right foot came up high and came crashing down with force onto her assailant's instep. Simultaneously, she flung her head back in sheer violent revolt and felt a hard surface give way with a *thwack*. She turned to face her enemy and saw a youngish woman, holding her face as blood ran down her chin. Through the fingers were a set of eyes, dark brown and narrowing as they focused on the woman that just broke her nose. Lydia ran toward the ravine. She didn't get far when she heard a gun blast and saw a bullet ricochet off a boulder in front of her. She circled around a big boulder and came up behind the woman who was pointing the gun at arm's length while moving toward the ravine. With no hesitation, Lydia leaped onto the woman from behind knocking the gun out of her hands, sending it clattering down the outcrop into the ravine. The woman raised both arms with closed fists and landed a blow on Lydia's head, driving her to the ground. Lydia scissored her legs around her attacker's ankles and sent her flying headlong into the ravine beyond the outcropping, smacking her head on an exposed and jagged root of a big cone spruce on the way down. She heard a high pitch yelp much like a jackrabbit's when caught by a predator and ran to the edge ready to continue the fight. What she saw made her sick to her stomach. The woman had a large gash on the left side of her skull and face that bled down her shoulder and into the sand. She was sitting on the sandy bottom of the ravine and not moving. Her right leg was stretched straight out front, and her left leg was stretched straight back with her left toes pointing up. Except for the blood and the foot, she resembled a high school cheerleader doing the splits at the end of a great play. She was mumbling something. As

Lydia climbed down the outcropping, she felt something fall from her pants and into the ravine. It was the gun she had stuffed in her right pocket. *God! What an idiot! I could have shot that bitch as soon as she attacked me!* She grabbed the handgun as she circled and stood in front of her mortally-wounded enemy. The woman was looking at her intensely out of her right eye and Lydia couldn't tell if she was defiantly daring her to shoot or begging for mercy. A dozen emotions and voices darted through Lydia. She heard her mother reminding Lydia to be kind to strangers. She saw Carl walking out the front door, saying he couldn't live with her temper anymore. She heard Dr. Karrington explaining that she needed to control her compulsive anger toward others and practice long-suffering. She saw Mr. Halloway demanding that little Bobby Sanders and his parents get an apology from Shara. She saw Shara crying day after day after school because of bullies. She saw Shara crying when being told her mother was kidnapped and killed by deranged psychopaths and won't be coming home again *ever*. She looked at the woman again who was beginning to wheeze from inhaling the blood running into her mouth from her broken nose and head wound. Lydia released the safety, raised the gun, said "Piss on Dr. Karrington. For you, Monica. Die bitch!" and pulled the trigger.

When they arrived at the Townhouse, it was a little after noon. Sarah came out of the bathroom and saw Ricki sitting on the couch frantically flipping through screens on her phone and looking pale. "They have Lydia." Looking up at Sarah, she repeated it, "They have Lydia. I have to go find her." Ricki showed Sarah the photos that Lydia sent.

"You don't know where she is, Ricki. You need to tell Don and McElroy. Or tell that agent outside. You can't save her."

"I *do* know where she is. These photos with GPS coordinates say she's north of Ramona near the Cleveland National Forest. She's loose and she's on the run with a gun. She sent the first photo at 7:30 this morning. Look, it's barely light. The last photo she sent was at 10:24. I texted back, but no reply yet. Let's go. You can call my dad while

I'm driving. We'll map out a way to find her as we go. It'll take an hour to get there."

The weekend traffic wasn't too bad on the I-5 as they headed north past the Torrey Pines Reserve. Ricki pointed out the golf course, peppered with the infamous conifers. Sarah left several voice messages to Don's phone, but he hadn't returned the call yet. Ricki wondered if their FBI tail was following them, and for the first time, was hoping he was. Sarah sent Mike a text message. Using Ricki's phone, she worked on finding the best route to Lydia. "It looks like Lydia took this photo west from this cabin near this ravine," showing the satellite map to Ricki. "Of course, we have no idea where she started or where she is now." Sarah sent a return text to Lydia, "Where R U now? On our way. Give current coordinates."

They arrived at a cul de sac in a run-down sub-division - the kind with front yards of crabgrass creeping beneath spider-infested vehicles, some without wheels and perched on cinderblocks like wing-clipped birds. A dirt road between two houses turned into a small path that led east. After stuffing their water bottles, a first-aid kit, some gorp, oranges, a blanket, bear spray and tool pliers in a daypack, they headed up the trail. Ricki's phone rang and she quickly muted the ringtone and answered Don's call. She explained the situation and sent him the GPS coordinates as she talked. He implored her to not go any further. She talked over him quietly declaring that Lydia was her friend and nothing he could say could stop her from helping her. "I'm not a kid anymore, Don. Sarah's with me." She ended the call.

25 War &

The bullet surprisingly went through the dead woman's head without changing her cheerleader pose. After the impact of the bullet, which caused her eyes to roll upwards as if looking at the bullet hole, the woman's head slowly lowered, as if in prayer, until her chin rested on her right collar bone. The surreal moment of relief and satisfaction quickly morphed into a moment of abject horror as Lydia realized she had just killed a human being. Instinctively, she located the woman's gun and used a stick to carefully carry it and place it near the body. She tried to playback the struggle to determine whether to place the gun on the right or left side of the right outstretched leg. She recalled the left arm came around her neck and it was the right knee that slammed into her back, so she decided to put the gun on the right side, betting that the woman was right-handed. She was practicing reverse forensics, knowing that the FBI and other agencies would be analyzing every physical nuance to compare with her statement. She retraced her steps making as few new footprints as possible and climbed up the outcropping on which she purposely bashed her left shoulder and right knee, ripping her clothes and leaving thread and traces of her blood on the rock. She then rolled in the sand to make impressions of where she landed and where she tried to crawl away from the armed kidnapper. When she felt satisfied with her story, she moved 20 yards downstream of the hideous scene, placed her cell phone under open sky, nestled into an undercut bank, and slept.

26 Outstanding in Your Field

Their pizza came, debriefing came to an end, they put away the laptop and notepads and unblocked their phones. Instantaneously, all three phones began lighting up with text messages and voicemail notifications. Tom cleared his mouth of pizza and answered while walking outside. Don's face turned pale as he looked at his smart phone screen. He didn't speak. He called Ricki. "Under no circumstances, young lady, are you to pursue your objective. Do you understand me?" After a few seconds of listening, he pulled the phone away from his ear with an expression of disbelief and said, "She hung up on me."

He looked across the table at Mike who was red in the face. "That was a text from Sarah. She says she and Ricki are at a place east of Ramona, hoping to find Lydia who has escaped from abductors. What the hell is going on? Where is FBI surveillance?"

Tom came back but didn't sit down. He stated to Mike and Don that Lydia hadn't picked up her daughter at her mother-in-law's house in the morning as scheduled and could not be reached. Don showed Tom Lydia's photo messages that Ricki had forwarded. Tom's anger pegged the meter as he stormed into the parking lot where he punched autodial a lot and yelled on his phone. Wearing a Hawaiian shirt and Khaki pants, he looked and sounded like one of those eccentric Hollywood agents who was about to lose an important star because his staff was incompetent. He was waving his free arm up and down through the air in front of him. Two mothers, with their pubescent soccer players, veered 25 feet away from their car in a half-circle towards the restaurant door. When Mike and Don approached him, they heard him say, "Yes! I'm mad as hell. They're finished. Get us a bird. Now!"

On the way to the heliport, Tom calmed himself by reporting some forensic results to Mike. "Monica's fingerprints were found on the window apron at the West Inn in Lake Las Vegas, thanks to Sarah's lead. Ironically, that puts Lydia at the hotel at the same time. The description of the man seen with Monica matches the description of Rousseau. We already have people on the ground, trying to pick him up. He'll be in custody within hours." He stopped speaking as he thought of the surveillance agents in San Diego failing so miserably. Don tuned out of the conversation taking place in the front seat and sat silently gazing out the back window of Mike's Jetta. Worried about his daughter, he sent text message after text message to her, imploring her to *'cease and desist'. His subordinates would do what he ordered, why couldn't she?*

Before arriving at the Coast Guard Island, Tom called Tanya to tell her that someone would be coming by to pick up his rig from the church. He also told her that her sister's case was close to being solved and the murderers brought to judgement. It was the one gratifying development he clung to as they flew headlong into an unknown situation with undetermined outcomes for three women in danger.

27 Déjà vu

Sarah was getting multiple text messages from Mike saying they were on their way via helicopter. She silenced her phone as they headed deeper into the undeveloped landscape. The trail was well-traveled, dusty and marked with dog poop for the first quarter mile or so. Soon it became littered with tree debris in a wooded area. There was a seasonal creek to their right that was mostly dry except for an occasional puddle. They came to some black irrigation hose running south, downhill to the creek bed. Both women paused and looked uphill to the left. Ricki started to follow it. Sarah grabbed her arm and pulled her back, "You keep track of the coordinates so we know when we are getting close. Can't get distracted. No one grows in January." Sarah took the lead.

It was close to 1:40 when Ricki announced that they were near Lydia's last GPS location. They were getting close to latitude and longitude coordinates that Lydia last sent, but the women were left to their own instincts to pinpoint Lydia's exact location. They knew they shouldn't yell out or call Lydia's cell phone because it might put themselves or Lydia in danger. Sarah took the bear spray out of the pack and Ricki unfolded the plier tool. Sarah veered off the path toward the creek. When she got to the edge, she looked up and down stream. Ricki came and stood beside her but instantly backed up. Sarah glanced back at Ricki and said, "Still?" Ricki shot her a *'go to hell'* look. What Ricki couldn't see standing ten feet back from the bank was the most disturbing thing Sarah had ever seen. She slowly raised her arm to point downstream. Ricki edged closer to follow Sarah's index finger. They were close enough to hear the flies buzzing in the silence of the sunny afternoon. Making no sound, they moved downstream, picking their way through crunchy spruce cones half-eaten by sciurids. Ricki was trying to determine if the woman sitting in the sand of the dry creek was Lydia. Her head was draped down over her right shoulder and big green flies were swarming the blood on her head and left shoulder. The woman was obviously dead and posed no danger, but her killer might still be lurking nearby. Sarah zoomed in with her phone camera and took photos. Ricki looked closely at the photos and shrugged her shoulders indicating she wasn't sure if it was Lydia. The hair was short and dark like Lydia's. Medium build. They waited a few minutes, pensively listening, while Sarah sent the photos to Mike. They moved to an open area downstream hoping for a stronger signal. From there they had a better view of the skewed body rapidly becoming an incubator for fly eggs. Ricki felt sick to her stomach, but Sarah was, as usual, not unnerved. Sarah pointed to the woman's right hand resting in the sand next to a gun. "Did Lydia have a tattoo on her hand?"

"No."

"Then it's not Lydia. We need to find Lydia." Sarah took more photos of the freak show in front of her and sent them to Mike with a note, "Not Lydia."

Sarah began to walk along the edge of the ravine, slowly eyeballing every root, rock and puddle, looking for signs or footprints. Something 30 feet away caught her eye and she pointed. Ricki came to the edge of the bank and looked where Sarah pointed. It was a cell phone enveloped in a turquoise case. "That's hers," Ricki said. Sarah abandoned caution and scrambled down the bank before they had a chance to discuss their next move. Ricki heard a high-pitched screech and fearing the worst for her friend, made a rapid descent into the ravine. Lydia, hiding in an undercut, came out pointing a gun at Sarah. Ricki started hollering, "It's Ricki, Lydia! You're okay! It's Ricki O'Conner!" Obviously, the woman standing in front of her was not Ricki O'Conner which made Lydia's face twitch even more. The crazed look on Lydia's face made Ricki realize that in a moment's flash, her best friend could die. Before Ricki had a chance to direct Lydia's attention toward her, Sarah raised her eyes toward the sky overhead and lowered them back down to meet Lydia's dirty, twitching face. Sarah made no other movement or sound, but Lydia slowly lowered the gun and sat down on a rock. Ricki watched in both relief and awe. *Crocodile Dundee.* Ricki took the first aid kit out of her pack and sat next to Lydia. Sarah took photos of Lydia and Ricki together with Ricki's phone and sent them to Don and Mike with GPS coordinates, noting, "Lydia bruised and shook up, but otherwise okay. Female assailant dead."

Don wrote back, "Do not go near the body. Crime scene. Take photos of Lydia's injuries before you minister any necessary first aid."

28 Knight

Agent Kingsley parked next to Ricki's car and called in his location, "Uncle Johns Court, east of Ramona, CA. Pursuing two females, Sarah Bolton and Ricki O'Conner, on foot east on dirt road at end of cul de sac." His black patent leather shoes were immediately covered in fine dust as he diligently trotted up the trail, following their tracks. He was in his late 20s and a gym enthusiast who avoided donuts and junk food while on surveillance assignments. He quickly came to the irrigation hose, snapped a photo and continued up the incline. Without warning, he felt a blow to the backside of his knees, throwing his body backwards and onto his back. The last thing he saw was Santa Claus overhead wearing a tie-dyed doo rag and camo shirt.

Agent Kingsley reached in his pocket for his phone, but it was gone. So was his gun. Blood was oozing from a gash on the top of his head and his eyes ached. He was surprised he still had his watch and saw that only 20 minutes had elapsed since he was struck down by Santa. He stood and leaned against a small oak tree, getting his bearings. He found a stick to help him balance and continued walking up the trail. The tracks faded as he moved into the woods where pine needles blanketed the ground. He heard faint voices ahead and rapidly proceeded with caution. He sensed movement behind him and flung around, expecting to see his new elderly friend. Instead, he saw Sarah pointing a gun at him. His clothes were filthy, his head was bleeding and he had nothing to prove his identity, thus he simply said, "Tom McElroy." Sarah lowered the gun and walked toward him. Agent Kingsley joined the women in the ravine and Sarah texted Mike and Tom that their surveillance tail had found them after being assaulted by a white-haired and bearded elderly male. Kingsley dictated for her to add that "his firearm, I.D. and communication devices were taken. Ms. Tankersley in possession of assailant's nine-millimeter." All four hunkered near the undercut bank and waited for the sound of a helicopter and boots on the ground. In the interim, Lydia told how she escaped and had possession of the gun. She explained she had assumed it was *Ugly's* and that she believed *Ugly* was shot in the cabin by the same bitch who tried to kill her, and she pointed up the ravine. "Who knows," she mumbled tucking her body deeper into the undercut, "He may still be alive and wandering around looking for me". Agent Kingsley placed his hand on Lydia's foot and squeezed gently. The small act of compassion didn't go unnoticed by Sarah.

Mike and Tom were relieved to get the text message and photo of Ricki with Lydia. Tom leaned over, showing the screen to Don who gave a thumbs up. The second text was less comforting. It was a relief to know that an agent was with the women, but unsettling that he had been attacked in pursuit. That meant someone was running loose with a firearm and they had no idea who that someone was. As they circled the area where the last coordinates were reported, Mike pointed down at three greenhouses on a west-facing slope. They landed in a clearing northeast of the greenhouses and a small structure.

29 True Force

Ricki heard it first, the faint chop chop of helicopter blades. It approached from the northwest and circled overhead. All four moved 15 feet up the ravine where it was devoid of canopy. Lydia waved her turquoise cell phone over her head. The helicopter appeared again and disappeared from sight as it landed upstream from the outcropping of boulders where Lydia struggled for her life. The women turned to dart up the ravine, but Kingsley hollered, "No! Stay!" Like obedience-trained dogs, all three women froze and turned towards him. He was genuinely surprised by their response and followed up with, "Let them find you here. It's all part of piecing it together." The four walked back to the undercut bank and sat down and waited until they heard voices.

Ricki hollered as loud as she could, "Over here. We're west of the dead woman. In the ravine."

Within three minutes she saw her dad running toward their position, followed closely by Mike. It was over. Don's arms swooped around Ricki and she felt her courage sink into his hug. She felt she might cry, thinking about how Lydia might have killed Sarah, so she broke away and looked into his face. He saw the pain and didn't know its source but was sure it would be disclosed over time. Sarah ran toward Mike. Lydia and Kingsley emerged, waiting for whatever was next.

After spending a short amount of time at the dead woman scene and conferring with the swarm of field agents who had arrived by ground, Agent McElroy approached Lydia and Kingsley. He shook hands with Agent Kingsley and commended him for his courage and dedication. He escorted the agent and Lydia upstream to a station set up to render minor first aid where their wounds were dressed while McElroy asked questions.

McElroy said to Kingsley, "There are a set of greenhouses to the west. We flew over them. We have a man that fits the description you gave, and his wife, in custody. We recovered your badge, phone and firearm in his workshop. You were lucky, partner. We don't think they were involved in the abduction, but we can't be sure until we run some data. They appear to be old hippies living off the grid and protecting their livelihood. Regardless, no more *Maggie's Farm* for Grandma and Grandpa." The Bob Dylan 60's reference was lost on Kingsley. Too young.

After Lydia's wounds were examined and found to be superficial, McElroy asked for her to give her statement. He asked Don and another agent to join the on-site session. Lydia told how she woke up tied to a chair in a dark room and managed to escape. How she heard a woman scream obscenities and then a gunshot as she was running from the cabin through the dark. "I followed the ravine until I heard a noise and then I climbed up there to hide" pointing to the outcropping. Still pointing, she said, "out of nowhere there was an arm around my neck and a knee in my back." She told how she kicked and flung her head back and broke the woman's nose. Pointing, she said, "Then I ran. I ran for cover behind those boulders. I circled around the outcropping and saw her holding a gun out in front of her with both hands, and walking toward the ravine in pursuit of me. I snuck up behind her and crashed my arms down on her. She knocked me backwards and I fell to the ground. I wrapped my legs around her like I learned in a college Jiu-Jitsu class and sent her flying into the ravine. She hit her head on that broken tree root there on the way down. I heard a chilling yelp from her and when I looked over the edge, I saw her in that position. She wasn't moving. Just sitting there. And bleeding. After a few minutes, I got brave enough to climb down. She must have been waiting for me to do that because she picked up her gun lying next to her right hand and fired at me. It didn't hit me, but it made me lose my balance and I fell the rest of the way down. There," she pointed at the rocks she banged her knee and shoulder on. "I had forgotten that I had a gun until it fell out when I landed. I grabbed it and took off the safety. The woman didn't move and neither did I. For a long time. After about ten minutes, I figured it was safe and moved down the ravine ten feet or so. I couldn't tell if the woman was dead or not, so stupidly, I moved closer. Her eyes were fixed like she was dead, but her head was still upright on her neck. Why would that be that way? It was so weird. Not natural. I took a few steps closer, which in hindsight, I shouldn't have because, suddenly, the woman raised her gun and aimed it at me, saying "Die in hell, bitch". She was gurgling blood and I shot her. I aimed, and I shot her." Lydia started sobbing uncontrollably.

McElroy put his arm around Lydia to console her.

Don was watching every move, every twitch, every reaction and added, "And then what?"

"I ran. I ran downstream and hid, hoping Ricki would find me. Or send someone to find me. And she did. You all did." She started sobbing again.

Lydia and Agent Kingsley were both airlifted to Scripps Memorial Hospital for medical care. McElroy informed Lydia's ex-husband, Carl, and his mother, that she was found safe, was headed to the hospital and would be able to have visitors after forensic processing. It seemed like hours that Ricki and Sarah were in the ravine with dozens of agents. There was a group of young agents staring at the dead woman's body and indiscreetly making jokes. Mike was taking photos and making notes in his notebook while Don and McElroy commiserated with local law enforcement and forensics. It was close to 4:00 when Don said it was time for Ricki and Sarah to go home. McElroy assigned a new surveillance agent who would drive them to Ricki's car parked in the cul de sac. Sarah was conflicted over being left out of the investigation versus staying with Ricki. She was relieved when Mike joined them. Don said he wanted the three of them to stay put at the townhouse and that he would pick up some dinner on his way home.

The new surveillance agent led them north along a trampled trail until they saw a cabin resembling a bee hive, abuzz with law enforcement activity. The sun was getting low, casting blotchy shadows on the cabin and surroundings so it was hard to see exactly who was swarming. Some were ATF, some were FBI, some were local law enforcement and SWAT teams. Black uniforms, green uniforms, black plate carriers, camo plate carriers. Sarah asked, "Is *Ugly* dead?" The agent turned, said nothing but raised his eyebrows, pinched his lips shut with his thumb and index finger and nodded '*yes*'. Sarah pushed for more information from the young agent but was unsuccessful in her attempts. Mike squeezed her elbow, slightly nodded '*no*' and pointed to his notebook where he had recorded facts he overheard at the ravine. They reached the agent's vehicle and as they drove down the cabin's driveway, Mike jotted in his notebook that the dirt driveway was located on Casey Jones Court, near Ramona, CA.

Mike sat in the back seat going over his notes. He glanced up when he felt Ricki's car accelerate onto the freeway and saw Ricki using the rearview mirror. Her irises were mostly grey with shards of bright green. He wondered if she had been watching him while he read his notes. She broke the awkward moment by saying, "Sarah here, was nearly shot. Did you know that? My best friend, almost shot, over what? AFPs!" There was quivering anger in her voice. "Two friends actually, nearly dead!" she added. Mike didn't know how to respond. It was almost like Ricki was blaming him. Sarah interjected, suggesting that Mike should interview them when they got to Ricki's place to get the whole story. Ricki inserted a southwestern flute CD and no one talked for the rest of the drive.

Sarah and Mike had several missed calls from Fogerty wondering *"what the hell is going on?"* and *"when are you going to produce?"* Mike offered to return the agitated calls while Sarah showered. He looked around the townhouse for a private place and opted to go out onto the balcony to talk. There was little privacy because the balconies nearby were occupied with residents sipping on cocktails, ritualistically waiting to view the setting sun which made the shadows of the palm trees lining the street stretch almost a half a block. The eerie cry of gulls heralding the end of day intermittently competed with Fogerty's voice. Fogerty complained that today's event was all over the TV and if he and Sarah did not submit a draft by midnight, they "would be fired". Mike doubted the validity of the threat but understood the sentiment. He relayed to Jeff how Sarah's life was in danger this afternoon, they had just left the crime scene, they have mucho inside information and that, more than likely, the news being reported is incomplete, if not downright erroneous. He conveyed to Fogerty the complexity of the conspiracies under investigation and how he could foresee a contract for a two-hour prime-time documentary. The prospect of an *Inquisitor* journalist doing a two-hour network prime-time report intrigued Fogerty. Mike reminded him, "Two *Inquisitor* journalists, Jeff, two."

He walked back inside where Ricki and Sarah sat cuddled on the couch like two puppies. Both had their hair wrapped in towels and suddenly he felt like a sixth-grade boy at a girls' sleepover. Sarah patted the cushion next to her and said, "Grab your notebook, or if you want to use my phone recorder, I have it right here." Embarrassed by Sarah alluding to his *Columbo* ways, he took her phone and began asking questions. He began at the airport, asking them to trace their day in a linear fashion.

"Who decided to go after Lydia?" Mike asked as they finished telling how Ricki received a photo text with GPS coordinates.

"Me," Ricki jumped in. "Sarah tried to talk me out of it as did my dad. No way. Lydia and I are colleagues and friends. She mentored me at UCSD and I'm sure she had something to do with me landing my NOAA position."

Sarah broke in and narrated how they found the cul de sac and hoped it led to where the coordinates were, "We got lucky."

Ricki continued, "I guess, in more ways than one. We saw the black hose and were tempted to follow it, but instead kept to the ravine. Apparently, Agent Kingsley wasn't so lucky."

"How exactly did you find Lydia? Was she not hidden?" Mike asked.

"Sarah spotted a cell phone laying in the gravel and immediately jumped into the ravine - like an idiot. The next thing I heard was a crazy screech and saw Lydia standing seven feet in front of Sarah, pointing a gun at her chest. I started yelling at Lydia that it was me, but I guess that only heightened her fear because she could see it was not me."

"How did you get the gun from her?" Mike interrupted still looking at Ricki.

"I dunno. Ask O.B. Juan there," Ricki mocked, nodding towards Sarah. Waving her hand slowly in front of her chest, she mimicked a hypnotic voice, *"We are not the ones looking to hurt you."*

Mike looked at Sarah for her response. She shrugged her shoulders, and said, "I just relaxed and accepted the fact that I could die today. I surrendered to my Maker and all fear slipped away. It just happened." Her statement was punctuated by a pronounced silence. Mike turned off the dictation app and looked at his hands, feeling like this was no longer a public moment. When he looked up, he saw a wet track on Ricki's cheek as she looked down at her glass of brandy. She had long fingers and her nails were clipped short like Sarah's. Drying pieces of reddish hair hung out of her towel and he saw there were strands of grays at the hairline. He felt himself being drawn to her fierce strength and bared vulnerability. Uncomfortable, Ricki popped up and walked into the kitchen where she continued, "When we were growing up together, we compared her to Crocodile Dundee, huh, Sarah? Remember the rodeo the summer before senior year?" Turning toward Mike, she continued, "She had mean 1200-pound bucking bulls coming up and licking her face through the fence! We got run off by the cowboys because Sarah was turning their bulls into sissies."

"This nature she possesses has not been lost on me," Mike said. "I, too, have seen it in motion and have been somewhat curious." He saw that Sarah was now uncomfortable, squirming under the microscope. "Sarah, it's beautiful, it's unique and it's you. I like that part of you. It makes you good company and, better yet, a really good journalist!"

Mike managed to hit his target because Sarah laughed and pointing at Ricki, said lightheartedly, "Go on, *B*. Should I tell him about your fear of heights?" Ricki sneered at her and returning to the couch with a box of cheese crackers, said, "Everyone is afraid of something."

Mike interrupted, "Why do you keep calling her Bea? Is that her nickname or something?" The two women broke out into laughter.

The hilarious chaos was interrupted when the deadbolt turned and Don walked in, juggling two full bags of take-out. Sarah immediately noticed the slumped shoulders bearing a near-horizontal neck – a posture referred to as *'the sinking horizon'* by Pilates instructors. He had lost a couple inches in height since she knew him in Sage and his upper body seemed to rest heavily in his pelvis. She looked away before he noticed her noticing. Don stood motionless in front of the door, looking at the three sitting on the couch. The image triggered a memory of Ricki as a teenager when they lived in Oregon and his heart swung into conflict. He realized he was tired - and hungry. Though he could hear his cell phone vibrating incessantly, he made himself sit in the living room, plate in lap, eating voraciously and laughing with his daughter and her friends. Sitting right before him was the only thing he really cared about.

They stayed up until 3:30 discussing the case while emails and phone calls poured in from McElroy. Don had an elaborate workstation in his office and all four monitors were fired up. Mike was informed by McElroy that he and Sarah could immediately submit an article on the day's happenings but not the bigger picture. They were to leave the reason for Lydia's kidnapping out. No tying in the Linden case. No AFPs. No ORNL break-ins. No mention of mercenary or eco-terrorists. Reporting the raid on the pot farm was okay, since the old man and woman were oblivious to their dead son's activities. The dead kidnapper's name, Michael Grady, was Santa Claus's despised stepson and the beloved son of Mrs. Claus. The Claus's real names were Samuel and Samantha Jones, rock band followers that moved to the Ramona hills in the 70's.

While everyone slept early Sunday morning, Mike typed a draft article for Sarah to edit, describing the abduction, escape and rescue. Included in the article were reporting of the pot farm raid complete with photos of the Jones', their greenhouses, the cabin swarming with investigators. Lydia's abduction and Michael Grady's death were reportedly still under investigation. Ricki and Sarah's involvement were not included. A digital edition of the article entitled *Abducted UC Professor Rescued near Ramona, CA* by Sarah Bolton and Michael Hadler was published Sunday afternoon, followed by a boxed story on the front page of the Monday morning edition.

Tom McElroy worked from the field office in San Diego where he received and disseminated forensic and other findings. Mike and Sarah booked rooms at a Holiday Inn Express and began piecing together an article that would be ready to publish as soon as they were given permission. Ricki checked in on Lydia via text message after learning she had been discharged from the hospital. Lydia called Ricki and they talked for a long time. She said she was under heavy protection and that Shara was in Las Vegas with her father. Neither felt sure of what direction life would take after this bizarre event. Ricki felt a familiar tug to let go of molecules and gravitate toward whole organisms – those living in the sea. Lydia, on the other hand, seemed hardly perturbed by what happened, and besides longing to be reunited with her daughter, was more determined than ever to transfer AFP properties into application. In Ricki's eyes, Lydia was dauntless.

30 Deluge ❧

Monday morning Don went to the gym to clear his head. The backlash from the threat to his daughter and best friend had caught up with him and he needed to work out. The texts and emails from McElroy and other investigators kept coming in, relentless in their intensity. The dead woman who attacked Lydia, and instead was shot by Lydia, was Rachel Carlosa from Costa Rica. Jean-Marc Rousseau, a Canadian citizen, was in custody based on his involvement with the Linden murder. He was distraught about the heinous death of Carlos, his significant other. As he was shown color photos of her broken face and ill-positioned body, he broke down and named several other mercenaries for hire and, also, those from Zimri Oil that did the hiring. Arrests were made in the United States of six individuals connected with pirating of intellectual property, abduction and murder. Four of them were Canadian citizens that were on the Canadian

Security Intelligence Service watch list. The CIA had been receiving information from the Canadian intelligence alliance, 'Five Eyes', on individuals suspected of mercenary activity over the last eight years. Arrests were made immediately in connection to the Linden and Tankersley abductions, but many more arrests were pending. Only one of the arrests - Robert Thomas Chaney, age 42 of Mendocino, California - had information about or connection to the Flight 1561 bombing at SFO. Mason Bailey, arrested in Maryland, who coughed up names of domestic eco-terrorists in exchange for a liver transplant had fingered Chaney on Friday. Under pressure, Chaney admitted to working both sides of the aisle as a mercenary for whatever job was for hire, and when things were slow, he would act on his own convictions in defense of Mother Earth. He stated that Timber Ashton, a colleague, had a plan to blow up a plane on the tarmac. Ashton had been tracing activity between an oil company based in Canada and a patent lawyer in New York. He said he had to stop them. Chaney said he had no more information other than he hadn't heard from Ashton in a couple months and assumed he died in the explosion. Ashton went by several aliases and used one to purchase his airfare and get through TSA. Chaney also stated he knew Reginald Bussy, the man who attended Monica's memorial service, now in custody, but hadn't talked to him in months.

The CSIS and other Canadian authorities, Interpol, Mexico's Center for Research on National Security, and the CIA had agents working overtime on ferreting out all domestic and international mercenary groups. It was unknown how many were involved in the industrial espionage case of stealing U.S. thermal hysteresis technology, but many individuals were targets of their dragnet and it was assumed that many cold cases would resolve as the dominos fell. The Zimri Oil company in Winnipeg was a small but growing company with many of their employees stationed in the shale basins in western Canada. The Winnipeg headquarters had been immediately raided leaving two hundred-plus employees immediately jobless. CEO Mr. Conway London Tilden and various board members were arrested and face trial and imprisonment in Canada on several counts of international crimes, including murder.

Jean-Marc Rousseau, who apparently had a soft spot for Monica, admitted his involvement in her abduction but claimed he did not pull the trigger and gave the location of a make-shift laboratory in Boulder City where she was shot. A nine-millimeter slug was recovered from a wall in a vacant unit of a commercial complex located off Hwy 93. Blood and tissue were also embedded in the drywall and expected to come back as Monica's. Rousseau was implicated, it turns out, in international money laundering and drug smuggling operations on the west coast dating back to the 1990's. Regarding the Ramona incident, ballistics confirmed Michael Grady received a single gunshot wound to the head by the gun that Carlosa had in her possession at time of death. Grady had also received blunt force trauma to the head, corroborated by the tissue found on the barrel of the nine-millimeter gun Lydia took - all consistent with Lydia's account of events. Ballistics also confirmed that the striation pattern of the bullets that killed Carlosa and Monica were a match, meaning that that same gun that killed Monica also killed Carlosa. Carlosa's weapon had two rounds fired, one recovered from Grady and one fired at Lydia but unrecovered. Lydia's shoeprints were traced from the cabin to the rock outcropping where a struggle took place and ended when her assailant fell into the ravine and was immobilized by serious injury to her lower body.

FBI Agent Kingsley, who had been assaulted by Samuel Jones, was discharged from medical care and making a full recovery. He received accolades for bravery and would be re-assigned detail after spending a few days at home with family.

Despite a migraine headache, Don spent the rest of the day in his office summarizing incoming information into one continuously-growing report. Tom called and said he was flying back up to Sacramento to meet with some agents flying in from D.C. and Langley, VA. "This thing is mushrooming into a rather big international investigation," he moaned. "Even the governor wants a piece of it," he added. Don was relieved it was being handled at the top levels now and not demanding his involvement. He wanted to sleep.

Tom then called Mike Hadler and said that he and Sarah could publish all findings thus far, no holds barred. He thanked them for their contribution and said he trusted them to do justice to the FBI and all involved in cracking the case, not leaving out the bravery of his agents. The one thing he left out of the conversation was that Mike's Gwynn was suspected of collusion with Zimri Oil and there were questions about why she and Mr. Auckman were on the same flight. There were no answers yet, but investigations were pending.

31 Divergence ❧

Mike found himself on a late February afternoon, gazing at the sun's reflection on currents moving methodically in the Owens river. He wasn't as intent on catching fish as he was on thumbing his newly-grown beard and letting his mind aimlessly float downstream. He had taken time off after he and Sarah published a two-and-a-half-page headline article tracing the developments and forensics of a complicated, intertwined case that read like a mystery novel. They had paid special attention to respect the mourning of all those, including himself, who had lost loved ones. The news of Gwynn's involvement with Zimri Oil, Inc. was a shock that he wasn't prepared for. Tom had called several days after the article was printed and told him about Gwynn's connection with Zimri. He also told him that investigators did not think she had sufficient knowledge about the company that had contracted her, exonerating her from criminal involvement. Furthermore, no connection was found between she and Mr. Auckman, the executive from Rangor Oil. Nevertheless, the news of her apparent involvement put him in deeper connection with Sarah, Ricki and Lydia. Now he was no longer just a widower mourning the loss of Gwynn, but intimately connected through her to a diabolic scheme spawned by diabolical people. Somehow, it made him feel dirty. Lydia's ex-husband in Las Vegas, a patent lawyer for biotechnology, was also scrutinized for any connection to Zimri Oil or other international firms seeking patents. To Lydia's relief, there was no evidence of Carl's involvement.

Ricki and Lydia both returned to work the following week. McElroy still had surveillance details on them but neither of them minded. Lydia worked fewer hours and spent more time with Shara who was being home-schooled by a tutor that Carl had hired. At work, Ricki ate lunch outside where she could watch the ocean and wonder what her life would look like if she had taken another path. She decided to call Sally, still living in Hawaii, to see how her research was going. It appeared that Sally was deeper than ever in biotech innovation for human progress. While eating Thai take-out that night, Ricki asked Don if he thought it was too late to change career paths. She was surprised to hear him encourage her to do so without ever asking her what else she had in mind. The next few days she found herself thinking about ecoterrorists and how they had been working both sides of the coin: capitalism and ecology. A nagging conviction that she was no different than they plagued her.

Sarah slept for two days after she returned to her flat in Daly City. She pulled the drapes and turned off her phone. She had a repetitive dream of Mark, Ricki and she running through a grassy field in Oregon, being chased by men. She saw the glint of binoculars from a boat floating in the swells and colorful scoops of ice cream. Bighorn sheep butted horns on a hillside above a lake before dashing in front of a semi-tractor and getting smashed to smithereens, blood cast in every direction. Human legs tangled in black half-inch irrigation tubing was a recurring image. With each recurrence, the tubing entangled the legs more and more. Then a river, raging white, would spill the disturbing mess of plastic and flesh into the ocean where aluminum fog dissolved its bulk. She dozed in and out of sleep only getting up to go pee and drink more water. She was processing through all the images and emotions she had collected in the last weeks and was annealing them to recorded images and events of her past. She understood all was being woven into a fabric known as '*life*'. When she could no longer sleep, she took a long bath, cut her nails which had grown too long and dyed her hair, which had become too dull. That afternoon she called Fogerty and said she'd be coming in in the morning. He was elated to have her back and encouraged her regarding a new investigation he had a tip on. She felt gratified that he wanted her to be a lead and suggested she also do an article on the mysterious demise of Torrey Pines. Mike and she were awarded a large sum of money as a bonus for the AFP story and were encouraged to take time off to reset. Hollywood was already making bids for the story and Fogerty offered to examine the options. Sarah was game for pursuing the opportunity but knew Mike needed time. He had much more to process than she did. The deals could wait. She went into the office the next morning to resume her life. The following weekend she rented a car and drove up to Sage to see her parents. She was alarmed at how much they had aged but didn't let on. They had become frail and walked with deliberate carefulness around the house – a house they had lived in for 59 years. It was obvious from their body language and awkward silence that they worried about her each time she alluded to the espionage article that won her bountiful recognition and respect in her field. Their angst saddened her. They had never dreamed that their daughter-the-journalist would be in peril. She worked on a few projects around the house that would make it safer for them and wondered how long they would be able to live in their beloved split-level home. That also saddened her.

Saturday evening, she visited Mark. He was stocky with a full beard and liked to ride ATVs and hunt with his teenage twin sons. She told about how Ricki and she had saved Lydia and that Don was still working cases and he was working cases when he lived in Sage. Mark seemed indifferent and aloof, offering nothing about himself, making it obvious to Sarah that there was no reason to continue the visit. Leaving his house, she felt ashamed that she regretted coming back to Sage. In sunny California, she was *'shooting the curl'* so to speak. Opportunities were arising, she had a positive life flow, and had finally started feeling strong and confident in her life and career. On the return drive home, she felt like she was crossing a bridge, leaving the home she once loved behind. Yet, she knew, with her aging parents, she would have to reconcile the two lands and work with her brother, living in Portland, on how to best care for them in their twilight years. She found a classical radio station and tried to not think. The redwood groves on the drive south were as spectacular as ever. Just north of Ukiah, she got a text from Ricki, "Don had a stroke. In hospital. Can you come?"

32 Appearances

Don's stroke was considered moderate to severe by the neurologist. He had bouts of non-responsiveness. Though his memory was intact, his ability for speech was limited and he appeared to have some aphasia. The doctor said he was surprised how well Don was recovering. Ricki sat next to him all day, holding his hand, watching the shadows grow long outside. She was not accustomed to seeing her dad in a compromised state. His face was pale and drawn even though he had a saline I.V. The hose of the canula hooked behind his ears made linear dents in his cheeks. The doctor had discussed with Ricki her dad's Advance Directive, which emphatically stated that no heroic measures, i.e., feeding tube, artificial respiration, transplants, etc. be taken to preserve life. If Don recovered to an alert and oriented state, he could override the Directive and make real-time decisions regarding his care. But for now, all there was to do was wait and see how he responded. And wait, Ricki did. It occurred to her that there was a reason that patients were called patients. There was a lot of waiting - *waiting* to have diagnostic tests done, *waiting* to get the test results, *waiting* to get to eat food again, *waiting* for the doctor, *waiting* for the RN or aide to answer your button's call, *waiting* for the physical therapist to show up, *waiting* to be discharged. And a person incarcerated in a hospital bed has only a clock on the wall to look at and *wait* while the world was spinning around them at breakneck speed. Patience was a premium trait.

Forty-eight hours after the stroke, Don began to move the fingers on his right hand. Ricki massaged his right arm and right leg and watched for him to open his eyes. Sixty-one hours after the stroke, he was alert and oriented, but his speech was affected. He motioned for a pen. Ricki brought a pen and yellow pad to the hospital and conversations became feasible. It was difficult to read what he wrote, and the lines sometimes traveled all over the page. The speech therapist tested his ability to swallow and found that he was at risk of choking, so food was not an option for him. Don opted for a feeding tube for a limited time of two weeks. He said if he wasn't improving and not able to eat by then, then he wanted to be on comfort care. Ricki argued with the doctor about her dad's decision, but her desire was overridden because of the patient's right to choose.

Ricki told Don that Sarah was on her way to visit for a couple days. Don scribbled back, "You 2 stay out of trouble!"   They both laughed, and Ricki saw the opportunity to ask him once more about the *'incident'* at Randee Point in Oregon. He waved his hand in dismissal to which she said, "Really, Dad? After what I've just been through with Lydia and international criminals? You want to protect me from something that happened over a decade ago? Get real."

"When Sarah here," Don wrote on the tablet. Some silence occurred and then Don wrote in shorthand, "What U do now? You considered job others?"

Ricki replied that she didn't know whether she wanted to get into marine conservation research or work with the public again, promoting the importance of marine ecosystems. "All I know is I want to work with larger systems and not molecules. And that I want what I do to be pure, only supporting good. Does that make any sense?" She noticed his eyes fill with water and felt compelled to hug him. He gave her a left-handed thumb up.

His demeanor changed and he began to write again, "Glad U out... No more AFPs. Distance from Lydia."

Ricki comforted him that whatever she did, she wouldn't be involved in antifreeze protein technology anymore. Don gave another thumb up and wrote, "Lydia = dangerous. Stay away!"

Ricki just stared at her dad, puzzled. He continued writing, "stay away!" And underlined it, twice.

Ricki was groping for the right question to ask, "Dad, I don't understand."

"Capable murder. she say Carlosa shoot her from when broken leg in ravine. No. Carlosa shot at Lydia up ricochet mark south wall of outcrop - struggle up there."

Ricki grasped the seriousness of what he was trying to say but didn't understand what he was getting at. "I'm not getting it, Dad."

It took at least four minutes to draw a picture of the ravine where Rachel Carlosa landed and the outcropping where she and Lydia fought. He used stick figures with tiny little skirts to show they were female - a detail that made Ricki smile.

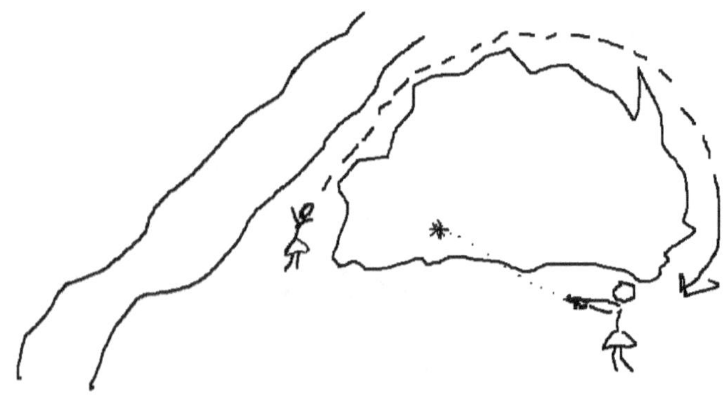

As she looked at the drawing and tried to make sense of what her dad was conveying to her, he pointed his right finger to his forehead in the shape of a gun and pulled the trigger. Ricki said, "Yes, I know that Carlosa shot at Lydia. So, Lydia shot back."

"U wonder why Lydia shot Carlosa's head? small target. why not chest? bigger target." He drew a bullseye.

Ricki said, "Maybe she has experience with guns. Training?"

He shook his head 'no', took the pad back and continued scribbling. "No. I checked. 2 rounds fired Carlosa gun. 1 in cabin, 1 at Lydia. Ricochet on rock. Up there!" He pointed to outcropping area from where Carlosa fell into ravine. He could see Ricki was still struggling to connect the dots and waited until he was sure she needed more help.

Ricki stated what she understood, "Carlosa's gun was lying near her right hand.   In the sand.   She had fired at Lydia. Soooo, Lydia killed her in self-defense."

Don did not give a thumb up but just stared at her through sunken eyes. Frustrated, he wrote, "I say for U. Carlosa not fire at Lydia in ravine. Tapping the pen on the drawing, "Bullet ricochet mark on boulder. Here. Up here! On top. On top! Carlosa's 2 round shot from up here." He tapped the pad again, this time hard. "Carlosa not shoot Lydia from ravine. Lydia shot head cold blood. Assassin."

Ricki looked at the drawing and it sunk in that Lydia lied about the events. Still, maybe Carlosa would have tried to shoot a second time at Lydia – who's to say? And does it matter? Everything Lydia had said corroborated the evidence and the authorities had believed her account. So why was Don telling her this? "I've always asked you to tell me the truth, and you have always made excuses. This is one time, I wished you had not told me what you know."

Don sighed and wrote, "I find bullet mark on top rocks. I tell no one. Not even Lydia. <u>U should know.</u> I'm glad Carlosa dead. But Lydia has a 'side'. She lied. Why? May have planted gun. Keep distance. Stay away." He tried to tear the pages from the pad but needed help. He wrote on one of the loose pages, "Shred." and Ricki nodded *'yes'* before folding them and sticking them in her pack.

33 Coming Clean

Ricki curled up on the couch with several pillows she brought in from her bed. She could hear the street below start to buzz with early morning activity. She wasn't ready for morning. She kept reliving the last moments she had with her dad – his strained breathing interrupted by long periods of no breathing at all. She held his hand and watched his chest heave and fall, his mouth gaping and his breath rancid. His newly revised Advanced Directive stated, 'no intervention'. He understood that hypoxia was God's way of easing the pain of death. His wife's doctor had informed him decades ago that pneumonia was called *'The Old Man's Friend'* because the buildup of CO_2 resulted in a sense of euphoria. To no avail, Ricki had argued with her dad on his Directive, saying that oxygen supplementation would help keep him comfortable. His condition had declined rapidly, according to the hospital staff. One nurse who came in to reposition the pillows under his elbows commented, "He must be ready to go. He's seeing his wife". Ricki held Don's hand during those last hours, telling him how much she loved him. She loved him for his strength. She loved him for his courage. She loved him for his love and devotion. She fought back tears and told him repeatedly that she would be okay and thanked him for everything he was and did. She resisted sobbing when she told him it was okay for him to go be with Mom. With disbelief, she had watched him take a breath and release it in one drawn-out exhale and she saw his life escape his body, leaving it utterly vacant. Before she drove from the parking garage, she texted Sarah saying, "Don died just now," and turned off her phone.

Two weeks later, sitting in a cushioned chair in the attorney's office, her skirt kept riding up her legs and she wondered why the hell she had worn a skirt. Sarah had dropped her off and would pick her up when she was done. The attorney explained the Trust and the transfer process. Ricki assumed that all her dad's assets would be left to her. She just wished it would happen automatically. But no, she had to perform a number of related tasks in order to resolve it. Thankfully, her dad's attorney had already been paid to guide her through the transition. Before she left his office, he handed her an envelope with her name handwritten on the front. She put it in her backpack and went downstairs to wait for Sarah. Once in the car, she opened the letter, read it and then handed it to Sarah.

Dear Ricki,

If you are reading this, I am no longer with you. I'm with your mother. You have no living relatives. You are alone in this world. You had a cousin, but he is dead. He got involved with a Columbian drug cartel in the mid-nineties. The incident at Randee Point you keep asking about? I wished you would've forgot. Derek was killed in a raid involving pot grows and smuggling on the Pacific coast. It's hard to conceive but Rousseau, the Canadian who was involved with the Linden case, confessed that he knew my nephew and that they worked together for the cartel. The mustached man you guys saw on the boat off Randee Point was Rousseau, and Derek was one of the men who chased you on the bluff. Now you understand why I kept the truth hidden from you. Derek disgraced our family. He was my brother's son and he had no children, that we know of anyway. Your mother was an only child. So, Ricki, it's just you now – no family. Nurture your friendship with Sarah. She's the closest one to you, like a sister. Never take that for granted. I love you so much. You will never know.

- Dad (02/27/2012)

34 Against the Wind ✍

It was early September and hard to believe it was still 2012 after all that had happened. Each event carried its own weight of relevance - the FFG kidnapping, Sarah coming back into her life, Lydia's kidnapping, all the violence and death, her unexpected loss of Don. As she sat holding a cup of coffee and gazing out the window at the trees slightly blowing in what possibly could be the beginning of the Santa Anna winds, Ricki marveled at how life's events seemed to bunch up. *You could go for years, decades without much happening and then suddenly all hell breaks loose.* She envisioned a river – a slow harmless meandering river – seemingly predictable. And then canyon walls and deadly whitewater, bus-high boulders and waterfalls. She thought *before you can even adjust, it becomes a slow meandering river again and you wonder, "Did I dream all that?"*

Sarah was arriving by train this evening. She and Mike. She was doing a story on the demise of Torrey Pine and she had convinced her boss to let Mike co-author the piece. Ricki had arranged a trip out to Santa Rosa Island with Rodney, a co-worker from Scripps Institution of Oceanography to learn about the effects of genetic isolation, climate change and fog drip. Ricki's shift from genetic research at NOAA to marine ecology at Scripps was nearly seamless thanks to Rodney, a colleague she had known since grad school. She was active in the aquarium's rehabilitation program and with the institution's ship fleet. She was happier than she had been in a long time.

Mike wanted to be present for the private dispersal of Don's ashes that Ricki had scheduled for Friday. Don's public memorial service in June, elaborate with photographs, military honors and 150 or more in attendance, made Mike a fan of Ricki's dad. Mike had bought himself a cabin near Bishop, CA where he free-lanced articles, some for the *San Francisco Inquisitor*. His thirst for the *'big story'* no longer dogged him and he spent as much time as possible wading in the benevolent flows of the Owens River, keeping a watchful eye on his fly floating in the film. Big orange moth-like insects called *October Caddis* were beginning to hatch and as he watched large fish rush up from the bottom to gulp the mouthful of flesh and wings, he marveled at how this sport had redirected his life. He surrendered to the notion of being an experience junkie and let his mind drift, not unlike the *Caddis*, on the river's current in the late afternoon sun.

An intellectual property patent for antifreeze proteins was filed by Carl Tankersley for UC San Diego, his unflappable ex-wife, Lydia Tankersley and the Texas oil company, Rangor, Inc., which funded the research. The scope of the patent claimed a stake on proprietary AFP technology designed to enable safe and efficient extraction of oil reserves in the coldest regions of the planet. Russian and Scandinavian enterprises were already lined up to buy the technology. Thermal hysteresis technology now allowed perpetuation of oil extraction in the otherwise forbidden landscapes of earth, a development that Neptune, Greenspeaks and other non-profit environmental watchdog organizations were vehemently fighting to halt. When Ricki heard the news, she groaned as she revisited her painful conclusion about the earth and its human inhabitants: *The force that propels people to kill for progress and gain is the same that leads people to kill for the conservation of our planet. How do you have zeal or passion about anything in life without becoming a pawn to this force?*

It was around 6:00 when Ricki parked in the Sunset Cliffs parking lot and the three of them piled out of the car. September was predictably sunny and there was an off-shore breeze that could have been the first signs of the

Santa Anas rolling in. Ricki, Mike and Sarah ambled along a path leading to an isolated bluff, sat down and waited for the sun to sink lower toward the fog-lined horizon. The grass was long and brown, and Sarah chewed on a blade as they watched surfers bob in the swells below. Next to Ricki was a carved wooden box containing Don's ashes. Her mother's ashes had been scattered at the very same spot 19 years earlier. She felt ashamed that she could hardly recall her mom's face or voice anymore and recoiled at the thought that the same thing could happen regarding her dad. Pushing back the negative emotions, she stood up and the others followed suit. She moved closer to the edge of the bluff and without wincing, looked down at the gaping void in front of her, opened the box and shouted above the breeze that carried the stream of ashes toward the setting sun, "I love you, Dad. Thank you so much for everything. I am no longer afraid". She felt as though that was all that needed to be said. Sarah stood motionless beside her friend, halfway expecting Ricki to say more. Mike shifted his position until he was behind Ricki, loosely draped his arms around her shoulders, pulled her back a little from the edge and rested his chin on the top of her head. She leaned back and accepted his warmth. The three stood motionless until the sun was well below the horizon. ᦓ

❧ Epilogue: No Shadow of Turning ❦

She moved along a path that wove through vegetation toward a hill that was as green as newborn leaves on an early June day. Colors seemed to vibrate with a brilliance that defied imagination, and sound, a blanket of co-mingled frequencies, made a soothing melody. Birds chirped in the brush. Water was running nearby but she could not determine a source. Beneath her bare feet was cool dust. No rock nor twig dug into her flesh. It was as if gravity was dead. Monica noticed a clump of willows gently rocking in the breeze. It had no shadow. When she saw that nothing had a shadow, not even she, she assumed the sun was directly overhead. It wasn't. There was no sun. Light was ubiquitous. She noticed a group of people walking toward her, smiling. She only recognized her mother and her mother's father, Grandpa Joseph. There was another woman - a young woman with strawberry blonde hair and grey-green eyes. Monica didn't recognize this woman who smiled at her in knowing and warm affirmation. A little boy was with her - a son named John. As Monica took in all before her, it became evident, *I must be dead. But I feel so alive!* She waved her hand through the air in front of her face. Brilliant particles swirled like a sea of fireflies. An incredible sense of safety engulfed her. Her mother's eyes emitted a love that she had never seen before. A selfless love - a knowing love. A love that encompassed everything. She recalled the realm from which she had just emerged and how she – how everyone – lived with the nagging fear of death, intimidated by its inevitability, and always - always - pretending it didn't exist. Always running from Death, running from Truth. Determined to be under the power of neither, they - *we* - remain ignorant of the forces at work. Fear now stood naked before her and she could see how all of mankind was twisted and contorted because of it. It forged all destructive behaviors from greed to cruelty to murder. Fear was a liar and a cheat. Fear was now exposed as a *Poker bluff*. A *bluff* that keeps humans distrusting the cards they hold so that they never live fully. The *bluff's* purpose is to prevent us from attaining our full potential, from fulfilling our God-given dreams - the dreams we dreamt as children before we started believing the *bluff*. The Bluff whispers and chants, "You are destined to be a failure, you are unlovable, and you are forsaken." ❧

"Look at the birds of the air, for they neither sow nor reap nor gather into barns; yet your heavenly Father feeds them. Are you of less value than they?" -Jesus (Matt. 6.26)

"For I did not come to judge the world, but to save the world" -Jesus (John 12.47)